CHERYL A. HEAD

JUDGE
ME
WHEN
I'm
Wrong

A CHARLIE MACK MOTOWN MYSTERY

Bywater
BOOKS

Ann Arbor
2019

Bywater Books

Copyright © 2019 Cheryl A. Head

Print ISBN: 978-1-61294-157-8

Bywater Books First Edition: October 2019

Printed in the United States of America on acid-free paper.

Cover designer: Ann McMan, TreeHouse Studio

Author Photo by: Leigh H. Mosley

Bywater Books
PO Box 3671
Ann Arbor MI 48106-3671
www.bywaterbooks.com

This book is dedicated to Aretha Franklin,
the Queen of Soul (1942-2018).

She belonged to the world, but mostly to Detroit.

Acknowledgments

Thanks to my Bywater Books family:

Marianne K. Martin, Salem West, Ann McMan, Kelly Smith, Nancy Squires. And to Fay Jacobs and Elizabeth Andersen for all the heavy lifting.

Gratitude to my beta readers, and content experts: AJ Head, Lynne Blinkenberg, Veronica Flaggs, Traci Tait, Angie Kim, and the Writers Writing Group.

And thanks, always, to Detroit for my roots, tenacity and swagger.

Cast of Characters

Charlene "Charlie" Mack
Mack Investigations Principal;
Former Homeland Security Agent

Don Rutkowski
Mack Investigations Partner; Former Police Officer;
Former Homeland Security Trainer

Gil Acosta
Mack Investigations Partner; Attorney;
Former Homeland Security Agent

Judy Novak
Office Manager, Mack Investigations

Mandy Porter
Grosse Pointe Park Police Officer; Charlie's girlfriend

Bruce, Brenda, and Jason Ferry
Mack clients

Maya Hebert
Rape victim

Gene Spivak, Karen Gleason, Earl Thompson
Wayne County prosecutors

Willa Harrington-Smoot
Judge, Third Judicial Circuit Court of Michigan

Allan Bateman
Defense attorney

Francis Canova
Defendant

Caspar "The Ghost" Goulet
Fugitive

Richard Fletcher, Mr. Naidu, Mrs. Andrews,
Clint Lakeside, Trina Bradley, Mr. Pizzemente,
Mr. Kelly, and Lucille Murphy
Jurors

Chapter 1

Detroit, October 2007
Friday

Charlie and Gil had an appointment with Bruce and Brenda Ferry in their Palmer Woods home. They perched on Queen Anne chairs in a little-used parlor with heavy drapes and delicate, antique furnishings. A uniformed maid brought crystal glasses of lemonade on a silver tray. Given the circumstances of the meeting, Charlie thought the setting pretentious.

Bruce, a judge on the Michigan Court of Appeals and grandson of one of Detroit's African-American, old-money families, worked hard at keeping up the appearances of his social status. He was a solidly built man with trimmed gray hair and a matching mustache. His suit was dark, his tie a conservative maroon, and his white shirt complete with amber cuff links. His polished shoes caught the glint of the Tiffany lamp next to him. Mrs. Ferry was tall and slender—delicate like the furniture. She wore her silver hair pulled back in a bun complementing patrician cheekbones and pearl cluster earrings. Although her plain navy skirt and white blouse gave her an almost schoolgirl innocence, she exuded the fortitude required of the wife of one of the city's prominent judges. Brenda warmed quickly to Gil, but Judge Ferry—diligent in his homework—had learned of Gil's recent difficulties with the police.

1

"Are you predisposed to championing prostitutes, Mr. Acosta?"

Ferry, who insisted on being addressed by his title, was as fastidious in diction as he was in grooming. When he spoke, his full baritone voice occupied the room.

"I beg your pardon?" Gil responded.

"My sources tell me the police were perturbed by your interference in one of their cases last year when you defended a transgender woman involved in the sex trade."

Bruce and Gil stared eye-to-eye for ten seconds before Brenda interjected. "Dear, you don't have to be rude. This man is going to help us with Jason . . ." She stopped speaking under her husband's glowering stare.

"For the record," Gil said without flinching, "we had a case that involved a dirty cop. The woman I tried to help was one of our informants. With her assistance, we identified that cop as a serial killer."

"Be that as it may, I need assurance that your inclination to assist vulnerable women will not affect your diligence in investigating the girl making accusations against Jason."

Two weeks ago, the Ferrys had hired Mack Investigations to dig deeper into the first-degree sexual assault charges against their only son. Jason was one of four men charged in the rape of a college freshman at a university in western Michigan.

Charlie didn't wait for Gil to reply to the demand. "As I've told you, Your Honor, I believe we should concentrate on proving Jason's innocence rather than bashing the victim."

Bruce slammed his sweating lemonade glass onto the fragile side table with just short of shattering force.

"An aggressive approach is required to contest these false allegations, *not* political correctness. Jason appears before a grand jury in three weeks. Maybe you're not the right investigators for us."

Brenda was on her feet dabbing with a napkin at the wet ring on the cherrywood table. She placed a coaster under the glass and settled a hand on her husband's trembling shoulder.

"Ms. Mack," she said "you came highly recommended for your

discretion and honesty. Frankly, with no offense meant to Mr. Acosta, we hired your firm believing our son's defense would have your personal, full-time attention. We hoped *you'd* be our point person in this work."

"I understand that but it can't be helped. I've been selected for jury duty on a case expected to take two weeks. Therefore, I'm assigning the case to Mr. Acosta. He's been fully briefed, he's a licensed attorney, and he's very capable."

"You might have mentioned my name to be excused from your jury obligation," Judge Ferry muttered. He was still agitated but Brenda had calmed him a bit. His suggestion was offered at lower decibels. Charlie was taken aback.

"I didn't think it appropriate, sir."

The judge looked contrite.

"Are you absolutely sure your focus on Jason, and not the girl, is the best strategy?" Brenda asked.

"You've told me your son is innocent of the charges against him." Charlie took in both parents with narrowing eyes. "Is that still your belief?"

Judge Ferry leaned forward in his seat, no longer shaking and fully in control again. He fixed a glare on Charlie that probably made inexperienced courtroom lawyers cower.

"I'm one hundred percent certain of my son's innocence, Ms. Mack. Jason would confide in me if he'd committed the crime with which he is charged."

Charlie and Gil shifted in their chairs. Teenaged boys always had secrets from their parents. But so far, Charlie's inquiries about Jason Ferry had turned up only a couple of youthful indiscretions—nothing criminal, nor sinister. Which was more than she could say for two of his codefendants. Charlie silently signaled that Gil should respond to Bruce and Brenda.

"Mr. and Mrs. Ferry, I'm well versed on the case, and the information that's available to date," Gil said. "Our continued strategy is to acquire evidence that Jason was *not* an actor in the sexual assault. The young woman—her name is Maya Hebert—was given a date-rape drug. Whatever else is in her background is superfluous to that fact. I know your family attorney, and others, are pursuing a blame-the-victim line of inquiry, but we decline to do so. If that means we're the wrong investigators for you, so be it."

It was nearly three o'clock when Charlie and Gil left the Ferry home, but it had been a good investment of time to ease the concerns of these top-paying clients.

"You handled yourself well in there," Charlie said, tilting against her Corvette. "They're good folks, just frightened for their son."

"Judge Ferry is pretty much a pompous ass."

"He's a piece of work, all right. But I agree with him about Jason. I don't think he participated in the rape."

"I'd like to go up to Kalamazoo to see the boy, and judge for myself."

"Fair enough," Charlie agreed. "Let's get back to the office."

Judy's color-coded filing system was lost on the temp from the employment agency, and the girl's face held a panicked grimace. Charlie had insisted on bringing someone in to help around the office during her two weeks at jury duty. She signaled a "have patience" look to Judy, who answered by rolling her eyes. The girl sighed, audibly, when Judy said she could leave early.

The Mack partners gathered in their bullpen to map out the fortnight without Charlie. It was space they'd shared for almost four years in a downtown office building that had been restored to its original architectural splendor.

"How did you even catch a jury trial?" Don raised an eyebrow. "Didn't you tell them you run a private investigation firm?"

"I did. I even told the defense attorneys I have a law degree, work with a former police officer, and quit Homeland Security. Still here I am. Juror number 540704, sitting on a criminal case involving conspiracy and bribery."

4

Charlie tucked her juror ID into her purse, leaned back in her chair, and took in her partners' stares with resignation.

"Well, at least you're taking on your civic responsibility," Judy offered.

"The courts really do need people to show up for jury duty," Gil agreed.

"I'd go crazy sitting around for two weeks," Don stated.

"Yeah. That'll be a challenge," Charlie said.

"What do you think of the temp?" Gil asked Judy.

"Oh, she'll do just fine. But she won't be touching my files."

"That's because you're OCD."

Don's statement hung in the air like a giant fart. The others watched now as he engaged in the twice-a-week ritual of cleaning his guns. He disassembled his two pistols onto a canvas cloth, unpacked an array of bottles and tiny brushes onto his desk, and used what looked like a short knitting needle to shove a cleaning cloth through the muzzle of his Ruger. He was oblivious to the similarity between Judy's incessant file organization, and his obsessive gun maintenance.

Charlie took advantage of Don's busywork to control the portable whiteboard. She drew a four-cell matrix and labeled each square with a case name. Two of their current investigations were simple domestic surveillances. Charlie hated these "cheating husband" cases, and they had been outsourced to two freelancers under Don's supervision. The third case was work for the office of the Wayne County Supervisor, doing background checks on two incoming director-level staffers. Gil had been the lead on that work, but Judy would now handle the required phone calls and document gathering.

"How did the Ferrys handle turning the case over to Gil?" Judy asked.

"Gil did a good job of answering their questions, but they didn't totally buy into me stepping away from the day-to-day work. Judge Ferry was clearly irritated."

"You have jury duty. Plain and simple," Don said peering into the muzzle of his pistol. "He's a judge; he should understand that."

"Maybe he could use his influence to get you off the jury," Judy lobbed.

Charlie shook her head. "He actually suggested that, but I wouldn't want to do it. The last time I served was eight years ago. The courts are always chronically short of African-American jurors. I just want to serve and get it over with."

"What time do you report Monday?" Judy asked.

"We've been told to be ready to work by 8:30 a.m. The good thing is I can park at the office and walk over to the courthouse."

"I'm out Monday, too," said Gil. "I'm driving to Kalamazoo to meet Jason Ferry. I've confirmed it with him."

"Well, I'll be right here," Don said. "Holding down the fort."

"And you'll be well-armed," Judy mocked.

Chapter 2

Monday

Charlie added the finishing touches to her makeup just as Mandy appeared in the mirror behind her. She felt strong arms encircle her, and a nuzzle on her neck. She leaned back into her lover's embrace.

A fit thirty-four years old, and five-foot-nine barefoot, Charlie always wore her curly, dark hair short for easy maintenance, but the style was right for her oval face and brown eyes. Mandy, six-years younger and an inch shorter, had a shock of thick, red hair and hazel-green eyes.

"You look good," Mandy said, appraising Charlie in the mirror.

"That's why I insisted on upgrading this bathroom light, so I could at least *think* I was presentable before heading out the door. You can't fix what you can't see."

"And what do you see?" Mandy said, focusing on their reflection.

"I see that we make a striking couple if I do say so myself."

"Except with you in that four-hundred-dollar navy-blue suit, and me in my brown cotton uniform we look more like I'm escorting you to a shareholders meeting."

Charlie laughed and turned into Mandy's waiting kiss. They held onto each other for nearly a minute. Then Charlie clasped Mandy's hand and pulled her out of the master bathroom. "I gotta get going." She lifted a small leather backpack from the bed and slipped into high heels.

"You're carrying a backpack with that suit?"

"Yeah. I want to dress like a professional, but I don't want to look like one of the attorneys."

"What do you have in there?"

"A paperback, a Snickers bar, my earbuds, apple slices, aspirin, and the report from the campus police on the fraternity rape case."

"I thought Gil had the case now," Mandy said, following Charlie downstairs with Hamm, their new four-legged family member, at their heels.

"He does, but the report came in late yesterday. I'm curious about it, and didn't have a chance to read it."

Charlie scooped her keys from the entry table and removed her coat from the clothes tree. Hamm looked back and forth between Mandy and Charlie, waiting for one of them to pick up his leash.

"He's ready for his walk. Sorry I can't do it this morning," Charlie said.

"I'll take care of it."

"Will that leave you enough time for breakfast?"

"I'll just grab some coffee and a breakfast bar. Should I take something out for dinner? Maybe fish?"

"That sounds good. I think we have cod filets and tilapia. Whatever you choose is fine with me. We can bake it, and I'll make a pasta salad. Don't I get a goodbye kiss, Officer Porter?"

Mandy stepped the short distance between them and executed a kiss that would last the full day.

The recently remodeled courtroom in the Frank Murphy Hall of Justice included recessed lights, high-traffic carpeting, and maplewood benches, desks, and paneling. The jury box had comfortable mid-back leather chairs, and plenty of leg room. All twelve jurors, and two alternates, were Wayne County residents, and among them Charlie counted four other black jurors. She sat in the second row between a retired custodian and a young woman Charlie guessed was about twenty-two. The retiree had worked for more than thirty years at the Detroit Recreation Department. He wore a sports jacket with shirt and tie, and was freshly barbered, radiating Old Spice. He wore a large ring with the Mason insignia on his right hand, and a wedding band on the left. The young woman carried a designer bag larger than Charlie's backpack, and wore the fashionable garb of her generation—fitted, calf-length pants under a geometric-patterned tunic. Her weave, parted in the middle, was shoulder length and fluffed, accentuating the large gold hoop earrings dangling to meet her hair tips.

"Nice shoes," the woman said to Charlie.

"Yours too," Charlie answered, eyeing the woman's red-bottomed boots.

The clerk, court reporter, and Wayne County sheriff were at their stations, as was the presiding judge, the Honorable Willa Harrington-Smoot. Their case, the State of Michigan v. Francis Canova, involved an elaborate scheme of kickbacks to Detroit city employees in exchange for lucrative city parking franchises. Charlie recalled reading newspaper accounts of the charges more than a year ago.

Canova was president of Fleetstar Corporation, and owned and/or operated a dozen parking facilities in the region. He sat at the defense table with a defiant set to his shoulders. He wore a dark business suit, and his hair was salon-styled. Canova's defense team looked like the big-money lawyers they were. One of them, Allan Bateman, was well known from his frequent television appearances.

Prosecuting Attorney Gene Spivak wore round wire-rimmed glasses over penetrating blue eyes. His fleshy face was framed in wiry, gray hair. He was assisted by Karen Gleason, a youngish woman with medium-length brown hair needing a good cut. She was too slim to look healthy, and her body type was more suited to slacks than the pencil skirt and small pumps that mocked her lean legs.

9

The first hour and a half of the trial was spent on Spivak's summary of the testimony they would hear from thirty witnesses, and the introduction of volumes of evidence. There were a series of letters, police reports, scores of memoranda, reams of phone transcripts, and a dozen depositions from witnesses the jury wouldn't hear from firsthand. Gleason's forte seemed to be document management, and she effortlessly passed along papers to her colleague that she often had ready before Spivak asked for them.

Charlie quickly regretted not having a second cup of the so-called breakfast-blend coffee from the vending machine downstairs. At the morning break she headed for the escalators and more caffeine, passing a handful of people sitting in the wooden benches along the courthouse corridor. One of them, a balding man with thick black glasses, had come into the courtroom at the start of the trial and stayed an hour before leaving. Now he was talking to a man whose briefcase identified him as an attorney. She studied the man with the glasses. He seemed familiar, but didn't look up from his conversation.

Following the break, the jury heard several hours of witness testimony—mostly law-enforcement personnel—asserting the authenticity of documents the prosecution had put into evidence. The witnesses described the searches conducted at Canova's main office and at several of his parking garages, and the type of evidence they'd collected. In a lull, when one piece of paper was being exchanged for another, Charlie leaned over to the retiree and whispered: "This is going to be a long trial."

When the judge gaveled a recess for lunch, the jurors scattered. Rather than sit in the designated jury room, Charlie purchased a third cup of coffee from the vending machine, and spread out at a table against the back wall of the main-floor break room. She read the campus police account of the Hebert assault, and sipped. Both the report and the java were disappointing.

The campus investigation had been woefully inadequate, and the local police follow-up not much better. Detectives had interviewed a dozen fraternity members, a few residents in the neighborhood of the frat house, and the victim. The report labeled Maya Hebert as uncooperative, noting that she initially refused a rape kit, and describing her clothing in disparaging language. Police had rounded up six Gamma members, including Jason, who had been Mirandized, charged with first-degree sexual assault, and released on bond within four hours of their arrests. Charlie made a note to have Gil find out if any of the Gamma members had recently quit the fraternity.

She glanced at the wall clock. The ninety-minute lunch break was over. The apple slices and Snickers bar weren't the best lunch, but they were better than the offerings in the vending machines, and had successfully counteracted the bitter coffee. She'd need to bring her own thermos of coffee and a lunch to survive this trial.

During the afternoon, lead prosecutor Spivak aimed questions at an employee of Fleetstar. The witness, Cornell Iverson, recited his well-practiced testimony which was made even more wooden when he paused to enunciate "collusion." Several times he swiped his index finger at the sweat on his brow and upper lip. He shifted in his seat and avoided eye contact with the jurors.

"How is it you witnessed Mr. Canova's meeting with Ms. Raab?" Spivak asked.

"I drove him down to Chene Park where they met."

"Can you tell us what you saw, Mr. Iverson?"

"Well, Canova and the lady from the city sat on a bench close to the parking lot and talked. Canova had the paper bag with the money on the bench next to him. Then the lady, uh, Ms. Raab, picked up the bag and walked out of the park."

"I have no further questions of this witness," Spivak said.

"Your witness," the judge said in the direction of the defense table.

Canova's celebrity attorney, Allan Bateman, pushed back from his seat, but didn't stand. He had Kennedy-style thick hair, gray at the temples, which emphasized his chiseled jaw and cleft chin. Charlie noticed the female court clerk and court reporter both had the same appreciative look for the barrister. The judge was unmoved.

"He's very good looking," the fancy-clothes juror whispered toward Charlie.

"Umm Hmm," Charlie replied.

"Mr. Iverson? Was Ms. Raab already sitting on the park bench when Mr. Canova arrived?" Bateman asked.

"Yes. She was waiting for him."

"How do you know Ms. Raab was waiting?"

"What do you mean?"

"How do you know she didn't just come to the park and sit on the bench to enjoy a beautiful afternoon?"

The question clearly hadn't been part of Iverson's preparation. He glanced nervously around the room, his face reddening from the neck up. He looked to the prosecution table for help, getting none. Bateman stood now, lifting to his six-five stature. He asked to approach the witness, and moved forward with a smug grimace splashed on his handsome face. Iverson sighed loudly, swabbing his brow, staring stone-faced.

"Do you need the question repeated?" Bateman asked.

Charlie watched the prosecutors. Spivak was annoyed by Bateman's new line of inquiry, and conferred quietly with Gleason.

The witness smirked and turned his shoulder away from Bateman. "Yeah."

The court reporter, using her transcription software, scrolled to the defense attorney's question, and read it aloud: "'How did you know Ms. Raab was waiting?'"

Iverson squirmed. "Well, when Canova sat next to her, they spoke to each other."

"Maybe they were just noting what a nice day it was."

Iverson didn't respond.

"Were you part of the conversation?"

"No."

"Did you overhear what was said?"

"No."

12

"How do you know there was money in the bag?" Bateman leaned in, glaring at Iverson.

"What else could it be?"

"Mr. Iverson, you're here to answer questions not pose them. Is that clear?" the judge admonished the witness.

"Yes, judge, uh, I mean Your Honor."

The prosecutors shared a look. Their witness's testimony was going off the rails.

"Did you *see* the money in the bag?" Bateman crossed his arms.

Charlie noticed that a half-dozen jurors had imitated Bateman's "convince me" gesture. Iverson looked as if he might try to stonewall again, then sneered and leaned toward Bateman.

"Canova said it was money. He said we were going to the park to pay off this bitch who works for the city."

The profanity changed the mood in the courtroom. A couple of jurors voiced shock, and a few more folded their arms disdainfully. The judge reproved the witness for his language.

"I have no further questions of this person, Your Honor," Bateman said. He paused as he turned away so the jury could see his look of disgust. If the action had been on a television soap opera, it would have been a close-up accompanied by tension-building music.

Spivak nodded to his associate, and Ms. Gleason rose for the redirect of the witness.

"Mr. Iverson. How long did Mr. Canova and Ms. Raab sit chatting on the bench?"

"They talked for maybe five minutes, like they knew each other, and then she left with the paper bag."

"Did Mr. Canova tell you there was money in the bag he took to the park on May 19, 2005?" Gleason asked.

"Yes ma'am, he did."

"What exactly did he say about the contents of the bag?"

"He said it was money to pay off the city employee lady," Iverson said, softening his earlier language.

"What's your occupation, Mr. Iverson?"

"I'm a driver," Iverson said, squaring his shoulders, tilting forward to grip the rail of the witness box.

"What sort of a driver?"

"I'm sort of like a chauffeur."

"You drove for Mr. Canova?"

"Yes."

"How long were you employed by him?"

"Four . . . almost five years."

"Do you know Mr. Canova well?" Gleason smiled and leaned closer to Iverson with each question. Charlie thought it was a ploy to demonstrate the witness was not threatening.

"Yes ma'am."

"No further questions."

Bateman fired his recross from his chair. "So, you were Mr. Canova's chauffeur. Weren't you also his body guard?"

"Well, yes."

"So, he trusted you?"

"Yes." Iverson glanced up at Canova and quickly dropped his head.

"That was *his* mistake." Bateman slung the words.

"Objection." Spivak rose.

"I apologize, Your Honor," Bateman said in response to the judge's glare. "I have just one more question." Bateman leaned back in his chair staring at Iverson. "Have you been given anything by the prosecutor's office for your testimony?"

"If you mean did they cut me a deal, yes," Iverson said, releasing the rail and slumping in the chair.

The courtroom was quiet. Charlie watched red welts spread across Iverson's neck. The prosecution had momentarily softened the severity of his cockiness and vulgarity only to have Bateman reveal the man as an emasculated, disloyal peon trying to keep himself out of jail. Spivak and Gleason stared at the jury box, as did the bald, bespectacled man who had returned to the courtroom after lunch.

The prosecution called two more witnesses, both tying Canova to a pattern of making cash payments to those he was trying to influence. However, Bateman effectively whittled away at each person's credibility. At 4 p.m. the judge had heard enough and adjourned the trial until the next day.

Chapter 3

Monday

Gil arrived in Kalamazoo at four o'clock and checked into an all-suites hotel that had free parking, a gym, and room service. Jason Ferry was to meet him at six-thirty. The hotel was far enough away from campus that other students, and Jason's fraternity brothers, would not easily run into him. The plan was to order dinner and go over the specifics of the case and the crime. Gil hoped the informal, comfortable atmosphere and the food would put the boy at ease.

Gil reviewed the background information Charlie had compiled. It suggested that even if Jason hadn't participated in the assault of Maya Hebert, he might have been a not-so-innocent bystander. Gil considered himself a good judge of character, a skill honed by years of work as a car salesman at his uncle's dealerships, and he wanted to give the young man a once-over to decide for himself whether the boy was innocent, or guilty, of the rape.

When Jason called from the lobby, Gil provided the room number and then stepped into the hallway to peer down into the atrium. He watched the twenty-year-old depart from the registration desk and move to the bank of elevators. He could tell a lot about a person from their stride. Jason walked slowly, but deliberately, and with confidence. He stood at the room's door to watch Jason step out of the elevator, pause to read the brass sign pointing the way, and move up the hall with the sureness of an athlete. Gil waved, and Jason reciprocated with an upheld hand and a tentative smile.

"Hi." Gil extended his hand, and the boy gripped it firmly. "Come on in."

Jason surveyed the suite with a swivel of his head. He walked to the small sleeper-sofa and lowered his six-foot-seven frame into the soft cushions. He wore expensive sneakers and nylon sweatpants with a matching jacket. His hair was cut short on the sides in a modified mohawk popular with young black men, and he wore small diamond stud earrings and a large sports watch.

"Nice room," Jason said with a nod.

"Thanks. I wanted to have enough space for us to eat and talk. You want to find something on the room service menu?"

After Gil phoned in the dinner order, he turned the desk chair toward Jason, crossed his legs, and leaned back. Jason already seemed relaxed, but Gil hoped the boy would really let his guard down.

"So, tell me about what happened at the fraternity party . . ." Gil looked down at the paper on his lap. "On February 18, where Maya Hebert was assaulted."

"What do you want to know?"

"Tell me all of it. Everything you can remember."

"I think it'll be easier if you ask me questions."

Jason's demeanor was cool and unflustered, but Gil could tell he was also concerned about making a mistake. He'd seen the body language a hundred times before when a customer walked into an auto dealership wanting to buy a new car, but needing to be persuaded she or he was making a good decision.

"Okay. How did you sleep the night before the party? Were you excited about the initiation?"

Gil let Jason wind up with the softball questions. He listened intently, prompting a bit at first, then allowing the silences to feel comfortable by smiling and nodding. Gil nonchalantly pulled a bag of Gummy Bears out of his backpack, put one in his mouth, wiggled the bag invitingly, and poured a handful into Jason's waiting palm.

Jason was talking freely now, leaning against one of the sofa pillows. He had been one of seven initiates for the local fraternity. The year before, the university had cracked down on hazing violations, so the ceremony itself was sober, but the celebration that followed was something different. Drinking and soft drugs were a mainstay at campus parties, and by midnight the revelry was in full swing. Four hours later, only a few guests remained among the fraternity members. One of them, Maya Hebert, had been drinking heavily all night along with her two girlfriends. Jason had watched two of his fraternity brothers, one on each of Maya's elbows, hoist her up the stairs. Her limp legs and feet never touched the steps.

"Why didn't Maya's girlfriends intervene?"

"They were passed out on the couch. A bunch of people were out of it and sleeping all over the room."

One by one, the new initiates were summoned to the bedroom where the barely conscious Maya was repeatedly raped while a half-dozen onlookers lined the walls. A few of the bystanders videotaped the attack with their cellphones.

"What did *you* do, Jason?"

The boy shifted position on the sofa, grabbed one of the cushions, and held it tightly against his chest. He began to perspire, and finally buried his face in the cushion. His head bobbed and his shoulders jerked as he cried. Gil looked away when Jason finally lifted his head and wiped away tears with the tail of his jersey.

"When they called me upstairs, I pretended I was too drunk to . . . well, you know. I hung against the wall for a little while, then played like I was about to throw up. I went back downstairs where Maya's friends were still passed out on the sofa. I knew what was happening upstairs, but I didn't know what I could do. I just knew I didn't want to be a part of it. When her friends started to wake up, I told them Maya had already gone home."

"Jason, why did you say that?" Gil tried to keep the tone of judgment out of his voice.

18

A knock, and the call "room service" cut short the interrogation. Gil bounded from the chair and moved to the door. He glanced over his shoulder to make sure Jason had regained his composure before allowing the server into the room.

They ate steaks with red potatoes and mixed vegetables, and shared a dinner-sized Caesar salad. Gil had ordered a large bottle of sparkling water, but Jason requested a beer. Gil hesitated only a moment before retrieving a Bud from the minibar. The two enjoyed a discussion about basketball while they ate. When Jason picked up his fork to attack a piece of chocolate cake, Gil picked up where he'd left off.

"Why did you send Maya's girlfriends away?"

Jason had shaken off the premeal conversation and was caught off guard by the question. He swallowed the huge piece of cake in his mouth in one hard gulp and looked up at Gil with annoyance. He pushed the plate away.

"I thought if they stayed around, the same thing might happen to them," he said angrily. "I wanted to get out of there myself, so I walked them to Maya's dorm. When I got back to the fraternity house, everybody was gone or asleep."

"Where was Maya?"

"I don't know. She wasn't there."

"Did you tell the police your story?"

"Yeah. I told 'em what I'm telling you, but all they keep asking is, if you didn't rape that girl, then who did?"

"And you won't tell them."

"Man, I ain't no snitch."

Gil sat at the desk, punching the keyboard of his laptop. He had preferred not to distract Jason with a lot of notetaking while they talked, but now he rapidly recaptured their conversation. When he was done, he had twelve pages—general thoughts about the case, observations about Jason, answers to verify, and other revelations he was still curious about. He was disgusted by the things Jason had told him. When had it become a spectator sport to

19

watch a young woman being raped? At what point had the reflex to help a person in trouble been replaced by the reflex to record that trouble on a phone camera?

Gil dialed Charlie, who picked up on the third ring.

"Did I catch you at a bad time?"

"No. Mandy and I just got back from walking Hamm. How'd the meeting go with Jason?"

"Good. He's smart. He has a jock's cockiness but also a sensitive side. A typical young man trying to figure things out for himself. He ate a *whole* lot of food."

"We'll charge the meal to his parents," Charlie said, laughing. "So do you think he was involved in the girl's assault?"

"No. I think he's telling the truth about that. But he witnessed a portion of it. Didn't try to stop it. Lied to Maya's friends and didn't report any of it to the police. I'm pretty pissed off about his inaction."

"He doesn't want to inform on his friends."

"So he said."

"That's also what he told his father, and why they want us to find another way to prove his innocence."

"I don't know, Charlie. It feels like there may be more to it than that. Not wanting to be a snitch, I mean." Gil let that idea hang in the air. "Did you ever speak to Maya's girlfriends?"

"No," Charlie said. "I hadn't done that yet. They're minors. Friends of hers from the local high school and weren't listed in the police report. Did Jason give you their names?"

"Yes, I have their names, and I'm going to try to track them down tomorrow. I looked them up on Facebook. I'm thinking about hanging outside the high school to see if I can spot them."

"If I didn't know better, Mr. Acosta, I'd say you were a letch. Stalking high-school girls is bad business."

"The things I do for Mack Investigations," Gil joked.

"Did you get to speak with the local police?"

"No time today," he said, turning serious again. "But I will tomorrow. I also plan to visit the library and check what the local papers are saying about the case."

20

"That all sounds good."

"Say, how was jury duty?"

"The things I do to be a good citizen."

"That bad?"

"White-collar crime doesn't make for much excitement."

"That's true. You back at it tomorrow?"

"Yep. So, keep me posted. I'll check messages during one of my breaks. Don't get arrested slinking around the high school."

"I'll be careful. Say 'hi' to Mandy for me."

"Will do. Also hello to Darla from us."

Darla Sanchez wasn't like any other woman Gil had dated. Like him, she was a third-generation Mexican-American. She was devoted to her family and proud of her heritage, and as laid-back as one of his basketball buddies. In fact, she loved basketball and most other sports—and cars. He'd met her two summers ago when she drove her 2005 Jeep Cherokee to his uncle's dealership for a tow package. They started dating after that. She wasn't the most beautiful woman he'd hooked up with, but Darla was pretty, funny, independent, and confident. He really liked her style. He realized he'd fallen in love with Darla this past summer when they'd taken a long weekend trip to the U.P. Gripping the wheel with determination, she had navigated her Jeep over the Silver Lake Sand Dunes in Western Michigan. Her tanned, muscular arms glistened with perspiration, her raven-colored hair blew around her head with abandon, and she laughed with the delight of a child flying a kite.

"You done working for the day?" Darla asked now.

"Uh-huh."

"How's your hotel room?"

"Lonely."

"I bet you've used that line before."

"Maybe I have."

"You're back tomorrow though, huh?"

"Yes. But late. How was your day?"

Their nightly conversations were catch-ups on the day, check-ins on family, and a ritual of the growing connection they had. Gil had witnessed this kind of fitting together only a few times in his thirty years. First, in the forty-year relationship of his mother and father, and more recently in the relationships his two business partners enjoyed with their significant others. He'd begun to believe that this kind of love would elude him. Then Darla drove him across the dunes, and he saw her for the first time.

"Charlie and Mandy said hi."

"Are they doing okay?"

"Yes. They have a new dog."

"Wow, they're really becoming domestic."

"Maybe it's about time for us to be domestic."

There was a long pause on the line until Gil said: "Crickets?"

Darla laughed. "Good night, Gil Acosta. I'll see you tomorrow. Love you."

"Love you, too."

Charlie and Mandy had discussed the pros and cons of getting a dog for months before they brought Hamm into their lives. Charlie hadn't grown up with pets, and her dander allergies kept her at arm's length from most cats, even the irresistible kittens Judy had brought to the office a few weeks ago. Don had adopted one kitten for his son, Rudy. Two of the other tenants in their building had scooped up a couple of the furry balls of adorable. But Charlie's watering eyes kept her from succumbing to their cuteness.

The dog debate had ended last month when a visit to the local pet shelter put Mandy and Charlie in proximity to a lop-eared mixed-breed who had a friendly tail, and soulful eyes revealing the rough times he'd witnessed. The compromise on a canine name came by using their first initials: MC—and, of course, Hammer had to follow.

Hamm lounged on a doggie bed across from the bedroom door, his huge paws splayed on the soft corduroy rim. In his usual nighttime pattern, he'd settled down to the soothing voices and soft laughter of his new owners; then, moments later he assaulted the quiet with his old man's snore.

"I don't know why Hamm can't sleep with us," Mandy said, adjusting the pillow under her neck. "There's going to be a thunderstorm tonight, and loud noises scare him."

"He'll be all right. I'll put the protective blanket over him before I turn out the lights."

"If we let him get on the foot of the bed now, you won't have to get up again."

Mandy's dancing eyes flashed the love she felt for all four-legged creatures. She'd considered a career as a veterinarian before her brother's death on 9/11 had set her on a different path.

"Tonight we'll let sleeping dogs lie, shall we?"

Mandy punched Charlie's firm bicep to acknowledge the bad pun, then waited for an outstretched arm so she could snuggle against Charlie's breast.

"So, another boring day of jury duty tomorrow?"

"Yep. We're being overwhelmed with documents. We only heard three live witnesses today. The rest of the time we listened to audio recordings, read along on transcripts, and watched a few video depositions."

"All that sitting's gonna get to you. Since your morning work-outs aren't possible, you think you should go to the gym before you come home?"

"I could. Or maybe I'll just use our treadmill and weights on the weekdays, and do the gym on Saturday. The one thing I absolutely *must* do in the morning is prepare a thermos of coffee. The stuff at the courthouse is horrible."

"Well, don't worry about walking Hamm. I can do that before I leave."

"You're a good helpmeet."

"What?"

"A Bible term for a partner who helps you meet your needs."

A flash of light careened beyond the edges of the mini-blinds, followed ten seconds later by a clap of thunder. Hamm rose to his feet, his ears morphing into antennae. He stared longingly at the human bed. Charlie rose to get the flannel comfort vest and secured it around his chest with the Velcro straps. The advertising said it was guaranteed to provide well-being to thunder-afflicted pooches. Hamm licked Charlie's face, and she gave him a rub under the chin.

"Do you need a chin rub, too?" Charlie said, slipping under the sheets.

"No, but I wouldn't mind a little spooning."

Charlie doused the lights and rolled over, pressing her thighs against the back of Mandy's. She draped an arm across her lover's torso and pulled her in tight. The storm's light-and-sound show eventually subsided, and the rhythm of their breathing, along with dog snores, lulled them into a contented sleep.

Chapter 4

Tuesday

The morning was crisp, sunny, and the sky a robin's egg blue. Gil finished a thirty-minute workout in the hotel gym, then called ahead to arrange a breakfast chat with Detective Candace Holt of the Kalamazoo Police Department. They met at the front desk of police headquarters, and walked a quarter mile to the Depot coffee shop.

Holt was tall, slim, with shoulder-length hair, and skin the color of café au lait. She was self-assured and aware of her attractiveness. The coffee shop was trendy—all chrome and dark wood, with a dozen round tables and a half-dozen booths. A haphazard photo collage of railroad cars, horse-drawn carriages, and buses dotted the walls of what the designer must have imagined as a hipster hangout. In actuality, the Depot was a stopover for a mix of city residents more concerned with convenience than cool status. Early lunchers ordered sandwiches, salads, and lattes to go. The decibel level rose tenfold when a group of chattering au pairs—charges and strollers in tow—rolled in like a baby parade. Gil and Detective Holt took their coffees and breakfast sandwiches to a window in the farthest corner of the restaurant.

"We've seen the video. It does seem to show your client in the room, but not active in the assault."

25

"Do you know who took the video?"

"Not yet. We got a call. An anonymous one."

"Can I get a copy?"

"I'm not sure about that."

"Will you check to see if I can get a copy?"

"Sure."

"Will you be the police witness at the grand jury trial?"

"It'll be me or Detective Stafford. Probably me though."

"Got it," Gil said, scribbling in his notebook.

"You have a rather interrogative approach to conversation," Holt said. "Sort of a Sgt. Friday 'just the facts, ma'am' style." She smiled, lifting a flirty eyebrow.

Gil smiled back. "I'm sorry. I really am. I'm usually a better meal companion. It's just that I'm catching up on this case, and I have two or three other things to do before I head back to Detroit. I appreciate the cooperation you've given. We don't always get help from the police."

"I did some research on your firm after I met with your partner, Ms. Mack."

"Oh?"

"She's attractive."

"She is. We're good friends."

"Just friends?"

"Yes. And business partners."

"I couldn't find any information about you having a wife."

"I don't have one."

"Are you seeing anyone?"

"I am."

"Serious?"

"The most serious yet."

Holt shrugged her shoulders. Her countenance changed from flirtatious to *c'est la vie*.

"What about you? Are you single?" Gil asked.

"Divorced. A year ago. My ex-husband still lives here. It's a small town, and there aren't a lot of men of color who aren't attached."

"Maybe it's time to move to the big city."

"I've got a little boy. He's three, and his father has visitation rights."

"I see. Well that makes things a bit more difficult."

"Look. Here's my card. That's my cell number."

"Here's mine," Gil said, sliding his business card across the table.

Holt looked at the card, and stared boldly at Gil. "I've got to get back. I'll check on whether I can share a copy of the video with you."

The Canova trial continued into day two with a series of police witnesses. After three hours of direct and cross-examination, the judge, wisely, offered the jury a twenty-minute morning break. Most jurors raced to lockers or cars to access their tools of communication, but Charlie opted for the spacious jury room.

In the area nearest the door was a large modern conference table with swivel chairs. A row of upholstered seats lined the wall flanking the table on one side, and on the other side were two worktables and folding chairs. The rear of the room had a couple of sofas, a few stuffed chairs, and two cushioned window seats. Charlie sat at the window looking out onto a small courtyard where the smokers gathered. A couple sat close together on a bench, puffing and talking. A gathering of four people standing on a grass border created a large plume of smoke that swirled around their heads. The others stood in solo practice of their vice.

Charlie understood tobacco's appeal. She'd been a smoker for a few years when she owned her first business—a public relations and marketing company. The high-pressure, long-workdays, no-weekends lifestyle seemed more bearable with cigarettes. But because she was also a physical fitness nut, she'd kicked the habit.

Approaching footsteps made Charlie look over her shoulder just as her jury-box seatmate, the retiree, joined her at the window.

"I used to smoke those cancer sticks," he said, staring down into the courtyard. "I was a pack-a-day guy until I came to my senses."

"Me too."

27

He offered Charlie a stick of chewing gum. She accepted the tiny wrapped rectangle and plopped it into her mouth. They both watched as two of the single smokers, their fellow jurors, came together to chat.

"Say, didn't I hear you're an investigator?"

"That's right. A private investigator."

"So, you like to hunt down missing people and spy on cheating spouses? That sort of thing?"

"We get our share of the domestic snooping cases, but we also do other work. It depends on what the client needs."

"We?"

"I have a team I work with."

"My name's Fletcher. Richard Fletcher," he said, offering a handshake.

"Charlene Mack."

"I didn't know private investigators were so attractive. You married?"

"No, but I'm in a relationship. I live with my partner in the Berry subdivision."

"Hmm. Lucky man."

"My partner's a woman, and I'm the lucky one."

"Oh. Hmm." Fletcher gave her an appraising gaze. Charlie couldn't read his expression.

The court clerk entered the room, cutting short the awkward conversation. She directed the jurors to return to Courtroom Five, and everyone began gathering their belongings. Fletcher gave a last look out the window.

"Looks like the smokers are done killing themselves. But who knows, the way this trial is going we might all die of boredom anyway."

Gil cruised in his Mustang along West Valley University's main road. It was a typical Midwestern campus with academic buildings centrally situated on an enormous quad. Residence halls and apartment-style student housing sat along the side streets intersecting the main drag. The autumnal light sparkled the leaves with color and gave the grounds a cheerful glow. Gil drove beyond the college buildings, dormitories, and athletic stadiums to the residential neighborhoods of the university's fraternity and sorority houses. He checked his phone for the address of Gamma Squared, and pulled his car into a no-parking zone across the street.

The Gamma fraternity house was unassuming except for the yellow-painted Greek letters mounted across the front façade. The neighborhood was equally commonplace, with well-kept lawns, mature trees, and three-story brick homes. A glass bus shelter marked the corner of the block, and adjacent to the no-parking area was a bicycle rack. On a bright midweek morning, the innocuous house on this quiet street looked nothing like a violent crime scene.

The campus police's final report on the assault was as Charlie had said—cursory in facts and depth. Maya hadn't returned to her dorm the night of the rape. She'd somehow made it to her family home twenty miles away, but she couldn't remember how she'd gotten there. She told campus security maybe someone had put her in a cab or driven her home. Gil surveyed the rooftops and street poles for city surveillance cameras. There were none. Several homes had security signs in the front yard, and a few likely had cameras facing the street. It was a moot point since campus security hadn't bothered to follow up on Maya's account of getting home. Maya and her father reported the rape to the campus police at six the following morning. Sunday. However, the police hadn't questioned the occupants of the fraternity house until Monday morning.

Gil looked at the campus map he'd picked up from the bookstore, and pulled away from the curb. Even with traffic lights, the three mile ride to the university police station took only five minutes.

Maya's old high school was a forty-minute ride from the campus. The modern complex included three one-story buildings and two athletic fields. Two parking lots were clearly marked—one for

29

students and visitors, the other for teachers and administrators. Gil parked in a visitor's space and stared into the lens of a camera secured to the roofline of the building. He had printed photos of Maya's friends from their Facebook pages, which he now realized would be of no use to him at this sprawling high-school compound. So he put on his jacket and walked through the front door. He signed in at the security desk and was directed to the main office.

During *his* high school days, no student ever wanted to visit the administration office. Being summoned there always meant trouble, and usually involved an awkward conversation with an adult—like the principal, school nurse or truancy officer. Things had changed. This office bustled with chatting, enthusiastic students. Some worked at computer terminals, some in cubicles, others at a counter with a line of reference books. A small cluster of students waited in an area marked with a hanging sign that read "Advisors."

Directly across from the front door was an alcove marked "reception" where four computer kiosks blinked a welcome. Gil stepped up to one, touched the screen, and followed the directions provided. There was a process for contacting students at Mayflower Hills High School, which was both efficient and secure. It included consenting to a photograph and signing your name. The kiosk transaction ended when Gil received a numbered ticket describing his request and the time completed. Connecting with Maya's friends wasn't going to be casual, easy, or anonymous. Gil returned to the parking lot under the careful eye of a dozen surveillance cameras.

His next stop was the main branch of the Kalamazoo Public Library. It wasn't far from the Depot coffee shop, so he picked up a chai to go. The library was airy, high-tech, and clean. To keep it that way, food and drink weren't welcome, so Gil sipped his tea at a bench near the front door and watched a steady stream of people go in and out of the well-used facility. He followed signs to the newspapers and periodicals section, which had an array of terminals for internet access. The staff librarian was a friendly, not-quite-middle-aged man with the demeanor, clothing, and voice of Fred Rogers. His desk nameplate identified him as Mr. Thornton.

"How can I help you?" he said.

Gil mentally added the word *neighbor*. "I wonder if you can tell me what's the easiest way for me to look at back issues of the local papers."

"You don't have to wonder anymore. I can assist you with that. We have only one newspaper, the *Gazette*. The last ten days of the paper can be found in those drawers." The librarian pointed beyond the terminals to a row of built-in counters.

"I'm also interested in looking at back issues of the college paper."

"We don't keep the hard copies of the university newspaper. You'd have to go to the Upjohn Library on campus to find those."

"Is the campus paper archived?"

"Yes."

"I'm interested in looking at the issues from February. I assume it's best for me to search on the web for those?"

"You're absolutely right to assume that. Here's the Wi-Fi information you'll need to log on to a terminal." He handed Gil a preprinted slip of paper.

"Thank you, Mr. Thornton, for your help."

"Happy to be of assistance. Have a wonderful day."

Between the *Gazette* and the campus newspaper, Gil found a dozen news stories and editorials about the fraternity rape—half published in the week following the February assault. The incident had prompted a maelstrom of protests, and calls for additional scrutiny of campus fraternities. Initial news accounts of the sexual assault offered Maya anonymity, referring to her only as a nineteen-year-old female student. But in April, Maya's father, Wallace Hebert, testified at a public safety hearing, making an emotional appeal to the men in the audience to talk to their sons about a woman's right to consent. After, that Maya's full name was included in the news stories about the fraternity party rape. In June, the university's new female president

31

announced she had commissioned a study on the prevalence of sexual assault on her campus. The resulting report noted a dramatic increase in the number of assaults in the last five years—many of them associated with Greek life. The campus police downplayed the accuracy of the report, but the university later issued a new process for reporting, and investigating, campus assaults, with a role for a newly-formed task force composed of faculty, administration, and students.

In August, there was one news story about preparations for the grand jury inquiry and the announcement of the campus police superintendent's resignation. It was clear Maya's brave action in reporting her assault had made an impact on the culture of the university.

Two hours later, Gil was headed back to Detroit with copies of the news stories and a tentative appointment to meet Maya's friends on Thursday. He punched his dashboard console to answer the call ringing on his mobile phone.

"Are you already headed back?" Detective Holt asked.

"Yes, but I'll be back day after tomorrow."

"I've been cleared to give you the link to the video."

"The link?"

"Yes. The video is on a website."

"I thought you had a physical record."

"We do. Our techs were able to make a copy."

"I see. Well, how do I get the link?"

"I'm emailing it to you now. You should be able to click on it from your phone. Usually the video will play automatically."

"Wait a minute. I'll call you back. I'm coming off the interstate."

"Okay. Call me after you've seen it."

Gil took the next highway exit and pulled into a gas station. He idled along the parking lane, and stared at his phone. The message from Holt was highlighted as unread. Gil didn't use his phone to listen to music or watch videos. He wasn't a Luddite, but neither he, Charlie, nor Don were up to date on phone technology. Up until early last year, Mack Investigations had used BlackBerry phones, the standard issue of federal agencies and a carryover from their Homeland Security days. Now they had the latest 2007 flip phones. After a couple of tries using his thumbs, the way he'd seen Judy do, he resorted to punching the small keyboard with his index finger. The link navigated to a grainy five-minute video. Despite viewing it on the tiny screen, it clearly showed the assault of Maya Hebert. It also showed a lanky, shadowy Jason Ferry leaning against the wall. Gil called Holt.

"Did you see it?" she answered.

"Yes."

"Good. We've heard there may be more video."

"It's unfathomable to me that people will videotape a crime but do nothing to stop it."

"It's a new day. People even show footage of themselves holding or using the property they've stolen. We've been able to nab a lot of people that way."

"Most criminals aren't very smart."

"No, but they think they are. You wouldn't believe how many people commit crimes they've seen on *Law and Order*."

"Don't they watch the part where they get caught?" Gil asked, sharing in the detective's laughter.

"I have something else for you, Acosta. We found out your client is a fairly frequent visitor to a club called The Apartment."

"The Apartment?" Gil asked, jotting it in his notebook. "What street is it on?"

"It's not in Kalamazoo. It's in Grand Rapids."

"What?"

"I know. It's a long way to go to visit a nightclub. Unless you're gay, and trying to be on the down-low."

The Mack partners gathered around the conference table. Five years ago, Charlie, Don and Gil, former agents of DHS, had inherited Judy from the previous tenant of their office and formed their company. They'd had rough spots along the way, like earlier in the year when an investigation caused Gil injury and emotional trauma. He couldn't save an informant who was brutally killed, and Charlie feared he might walk away from investigations work. Somehow, he'd managed to come to grips with his internal conflicts. He never talked about how.

Now, Charlie listened intently as Gil described recent revelations in the Ferry case.

"I spoke by phone with Maya's high school friends. They were interviewed only once by the campus police; otherwise, they've tried to stay below the radar. But they told me a few things," Gil said, looking at his notes. "They were very excited to be going to their first college party, but they were underage and their parents thought they were doing a sleepover with Maya. They didn't know any of the people at the fraternity party, but they met lots of boys and they had a lot to drink. They don't remember passing out, but they do remember waking up in the living room, and Jason telling them Maya had already left the party. They confirmed that Jason walked them to Maya's dorm, but the building was locked, and without Maya they couldn't get in. They went to an all-night diner for a few hours, then went home in the morning."

"Did Maya tell them what happened?" Charlie asked.

"Yeah. But they wouldn't talk about it. At least not on the phone."

"What about the local police? Did you speak with them?" Don asked.

"I met with Candace Holt. Charlie's met her. She's a detective and has been very helpful, but the campus cops have jurisdiction in the investigation."

"Here's the report they filed," Charlie said, shoving a folder toward Don. "They did the basics, nothing extra."

"Charlie, I sat outside the fraternity house today. Some of the houses have security signs, and I bet that includes some cameras. There was sure to be some footage of the comings and goings at the house that night, but I don't think the campus police ever looked into it. If they did, the information wasn't in the report."

"It was a sloppy investigation all right. Or maybe just half-hearted."

"I think somebody agreed with you, because the head of campus security resigned in late summer."

"I didn't know that," Charlie said.

"I have a lead on some new evidence," Gil added. "I've already told the Ferrys about it—a video that might exonerate Jason. It's posted to a social media website used by the college kids. Something called Flickr."

"Never heard of it," Charlie said.

"Neither had I. I can't keep up with all that stuff. I'm meeting with Maya's friends Thursday, and I'm hoping they can fill me in on what this Flickr thing does."

"The Ferrys must have been delighted to hear about the video."

"Mrs. Ferry was. Of course, the judge wouldn't show it. He's a hard man to please," Gil said, shaking his head. "It's gotta be tough for Jason to live up to that man's standards."

"What's he like?" Don asked.

"The judge?"

"No. The kid. He's a star athlete, isn't he?"

"Basketball player. Good student, and well-liked on campus. He's a good-looking kid. Maya's friends got all giggly when they talked about him."

"Does he have a girlfriend?" Judy asked.

"Probably a lot of them," Charlie responded. "He carries himself like a guy who grew up in privilege. He's pretty sure of himself, don't you think, Gil?"

"Yes. And no. He broke down when I pressed him on why he didn't try to help Maya. He didn't have an answer."

"His folks insist it's because he doesn't want to be the one to rat out his fraternity brothers," Charlie said.

"Makes sense," Don said. "I can respect it. Loyalty and all that."

"I've got one more thing." Gil looked at his notebook, flipped through a few pages, and then closed it. "I'm not sure what to do with it. Detective Holt implied that Jason might be gay."

"What?" Charlie was incredulous.

"I'll be damned," said Don.

"How would she know that?" Charlie asked.

"Before the campus police discouraged Kalamazoo PD's involvement, Holt and her partner investigated all the Gamma Squared members charged with the rape. Holt says Jason frequents a gay bar in Grand Rapids."

The overhead light flickered. Charlie reached for her sticky notes and the Ferry folder. She jotted something on one of the green notes and stuck it in the folder.

"Judge Ferry won't like that information," Charlie stated.

"Even if it gets his son off the hook?" asked Judy.

"No," Charlie and Gil answered in unison.

"Besides, being gay doesn't necessarily mean Jason couldn't be involved in the frat party rape," Charlie said.

"I guess not." Judy nodded.

"Especially if he's trying to fit in with the boys and hide his sexuality," Gil added. "I'll call Jason tomorrow. Maybe arrange to talk to him in person. He's probably deathly afraid of his father finding out he's gay. I can tell you firsthand, it's no fun to be on Judge Ferry's bad side. I bet Jason already knows what that feels like."

The Mack partners finished their meeting with an update on the surveillance cases—a husband intent on proving his wife's infidelity; a wife seeking the whereabouts of her husband's mistress; and an insurance company wanting to avoid a big cash payout on what they believed to be a fraudulent claim.

"All those investigations are going smoothly," Don reported. "No problems at all with the subcontractors. We also got a call today about taking on another case. A lady who's trying to track down her ex-husband so she can get his name off the deed of her house."

Charlie gave Don a knowing stare. Her eyes filled with boredom and disdain.

"I know you hate 'em, Mack. But they keep the cash coming in the door."

"Don's right about that. The domestic cases have brought in more than a fifth of our income this year," Judy said.

"The numbers don't lie, Mack," Don added.

"Whatever," Charlie said.

"Anything shaking at the courthouse?" Gil asked.

"Another mostly tedious day, but the defense attorney is Allan Bateman. He's provided a few minutes of entertainment."

"Oooh. He's that good-looking blond lawyer who's on TV all the time," Judy purred. "If things got dull, I'd just gape at him."

"Many of the female jurors, one or two of the men, and the lady court reporter and clerk agree with you, Judy. Look, I'm back at it at eight in the morning, so unless there's something else to discuss, I'm done."

"Do we meet tomorrow when they let you out?" Judy asked.

"Only if something new comes up. I'll check in during one of my breaks."

Chapter 5

Wednesday

Day three of Charlie's civic duty included listening to back-to-back audio recordings, and reading transcripts. After lunch, the court clerk announced that jurors would work until 6 p.m. to hear a last-minute witness. The groans in the jury room turned to cheers when she also announced that, because prosecutors had to attend to an emergency in an appellate case, jurors would have tomorrow off. At the afternoon break Charlie retreated to the solace of the window seat to decompress from the courtroom's penetrating fluorescents and the monotonous transcripts. She poured coffee from her thermos and stared down at the courtyard. The flirtatious Mr. Fletcher was now among the smokers, obviously having reversed his quitter's status. Fletcher and three other jurors formed a tight circle at the edge of the patio. At one point he looked up, and Charlie instinctively pulled back from the pane. She turned away from the window to take in the jury room.

Sitting at the conference table, an older lady knitted what appeared to be an afghan. Skeins of yarn and needles protruded from the canvas bag in front of her. From an earlier conversation, Charlie knew the woman had been a teacher in the Detroit public schools and had known her mother, Ernestine, a former high school principal. One of the alternate jurors was asleep on the sofa. The only other person in the room was the youngest juror on the trial, a twenty-something guy from Bloomfield Hills. The kid was hunched over a thick book at one of the worktables. Charlie strolled toward the young man with curiosity.

"I'm surprised you still want to read after the day we've had with those transcripts."

He looked up, removed his glasses, and pinched the skin between his eyes. "I have to study. I'm taking the LSAT this weekend. I'm thrilled to be off tomorrow to have an extra day to prepare."

Charlie peered over his shoulder at the text on his desk. "Ah. The PowerScore bible. I used that one, and the Kaplan book."

"You're an attorney?"

"Yes. But don't practice. I keep up my certifications and renewals. I'm Charlie, by the way."

"Clint. My father's an attorney. My mother too."

"And you're following in their footsteps?"

"Something like that. They gave me a year after college to try my hand at being a working musician. I milked it for another six months, but since they're paying my rent and most of my other expenses, I felt I owed it to them to take the LSAT and try to do well."

"I get it." Charlie held up her thermos. "Would you like some coffee? It already has cream and sugar."

"No thanks, I get my caffeine from Mountain Dew or energy drinks."

The late witness in the trial was Canova's former accountant. Former, because he'd spent the last two months as a guest of the state prison on the east side of Detroit. Prisoners usually came to court in their state-issue blue uniforms with the orange band sewn across the shoulders, but the accountant had been given the privilege of dressing like a civilian. Harvey Rush wore plain black cotton slacks, a white polo shirt, and a black cotton jacket. The man's bulging eyes, narrow nose, and long neck reminded Charlie

39

of a weasel. He fidgeted and constantly wrung his hands, but was a very effective prosecution witness.

"What's your occupation, Mr. Rush?" Gene Spivak asked.

"I'm a CPA. Well, I used to be."

"And did you work for Mr. Canova in that capacity?"

"Yes."

"How long did you work for Mr. Canova?"

"From 1997 to a year ago."

"Please describe the kind of work you did."

"I took care of all Frank's taxes. I filled out the forms, kept all his receipts, and gathered the other documents. He had a few overseas cash transfers, and I managed those. I set up his accounts payable and receivable ledgers. His bank statements came to me."

"Frank is Mr. Canova?"

"Uh, yes. Sorry."

"Did you make bank deposits for Mr. Canova?"

"I made the electronic check deposits and transfers. A girl in the office handled the cash deposits. I also worked closely with her."

"What is her name?"

"That's Ms. Kendra Vaile."

"Did Mr. Canova keep a lot of cash on hand?"

"He has a cash business. So, yes, there was a lot of currency moving around. But we had security protocols in place."

"Could Mr. Canova have kept cash off the books that you wouldn't know about?"

"Well, yeah, that could easily happen."

"Mr. Rush, can you tell me why you are currently incarcerated?"

"I was convicted of fraud six months ago for failing to report cash transactions to our outside auditor."

The testimony went on like that for a while. The CPA admitted he had systematically fudged the books of the Fleetstar company, hidden cash transactions, and filed false tax records. Allan Bateman's cross-examination focused on what Canova

40

knew of Rush's illegal activities. In the end, it came down to whether to believe a convicted crook's word against an alleged crook.

At six, the judge adjourned for the day, and Charlie gathered her phone and laptop from a downstairs locker. She'd left her Corvette parked in the reserved space of the building where Mack Investigations had their office, and after sitting all day she was looking forward to the walk.

There was a break in traffic on Gratiot, and as she darted across the street she noticed the bald man she'd seen at the courthouse. He was sitting in a parked car. He quickly dipped his head when she looked his way. Charlie's sixth sense tapped her shoulder. She walked a couple of blocks toward downtown, then doubled back to the courthouse. At the corner—out of the man's line of sight—she aimed her cell phone camera at the driver's window. Before she took a second photo, she depressed the keypad, as Judy had shown her, to zoom in on his face.

Chapter 6

Thursday

It felt good to be sitting in her chair again in the office of the firm that bore her name. Charlie traced her finger along the top drawer and the brass pull of what had been her father's desk. Judy, or maybe it was the temp, had dusted the mahogany surface during her three days away from the office.

Throughout high school, Charlie thought she'd become a lawyer like her father, but in college her ambitions took a back seat to pleasure. She managed to get her degree, but the bulk of her pursuits focused on serious partying, travel, and sexcapades. After graduation, and a variety of jobs including small-business ownership, she finally applied to law school. Not to honor the memory of her father, but because she'd been in the midst of a divorce and needed to demonstrate to herself that she could turn in a new direction.

"You're here early," Judy said, turning on the overhead lights. "Couldn't wait to get back to work?"

"You wouldn't believe how good it feels not to have jury duty today. I gave Mandy a break from all the morning duties. I walked the dog, picked up the yard, took out the trash, and made her lunch."

"Good for you. Family life suits you."

Judy placed a handful of pink telephone messages and a folder

42

with checks to be signed in front of Charlie, then headed back to her own work space in the anteroom. Charlie followed.

"I've gotten used to being ready to work by eight-thirty," Charlie admitted.

"But it seems like you're ready to be done with jury duty."

"No, not really. It's dull when there are a lot of transcripts, but some of the witness testimony is really interesting, and you know me, I love observing all the personalities."

Charlie flopped into Judy's side chair. "When's the temp coming in?"

"Her name's Tamela. She'll be in at nine-thirty, and she's doing a good job—answering phones, ordering supplies, sorting the mail. Gil has her transferring his notes on the Ferry case into a database he set up. Yesterday, Don asked her to sit in on a meeting with the subs to take notes on the surveillance cases."

"Great. What have *you* been doing? Let me guess. Filing."

"*Not a day goes by; not a single day,*" Judy sang. "*Filing's not a part of my life; and it's here to stay.*"

Within seconds, Charlie picked up Judy's parody of the song from Sondheim's *Merrily We Roll Along*. She started in on the next stanza.

"*As the days go by I keep thinking when does it end? Where's the day you'll have started forgetting.*"

Judy finished with, "*But I just go on filing and sweating.*"

They giggled, did a high-five, and complimented each other on their wit.

"Does Mandy know Broadway musicals like you do?"

"No. She usually smiles and leaves the room if I start singing. But Hamm likes it."

"That's the wonderful thing about dogs. No judgment."

"They also know good singing when they hear it," Charlie added cheerily.

Suddenly, Don rushed through the door as if executing a drug bust. Charlie and Judy's frivolity dropped like a jar of jam crashing onto the kitchen floor. He gave his office mates a "what?" look, then slammed the door and flung his raincoat on the clothes tree.

"What were you guys talking about?"

"Good morning to you, too," Judy said leaning back in her chair.

"Yeah. Good morning. What's going on?"

"Show tunes," Charlie said, grinning.

"Glad I missed that. No jury duty?"

"Not today. Starts again tomorrow."

"That Canova guy is a real creep," Don offered out of the blue.

"I'm not really supposed to talk about the case."

"Right," Don sneered. "When's Tate coming in?" He tossed the question at Judy.

"*Tamela* will be in at nine-thirty," Judy responded icily.

"Are you two like this even when I'm not around?" Charlie asked.

"Like what?" Don and Judy almost responded in tandem.

Don headed for his desk. Charlie waggled her head and returned to the office bullpen. She watched Don loop his sports jacket over the back of his chair, remove the gun from his holster, and put it in his top drawer.

"How are Rita and Rudy?" she asked.

"Good. How's Mandy?"

"She's doing great. There have been rumors swirling around the department about layoffs, but with her seniority she thinks she'll be all right."

"Hmm," Don responded, shuffling through papers on his desk.

"We'll do case updates this afternoon when Gil gets back from Kalamazoo."

"Fine," Don said, not looking up.

Charlie returned to the anteroom and leaned over Judy's desk. "What's with him?" she whispered. Judy gave a head shake and a shrug.

Gil met Maya's friends at a neighborhood park about a half mile from their high school. The square-block green space was well maintained with different sections to accommodate the needs of the community. There was a picnic area, a playground, and a skateboard park that could be configured into an amphitheater. A woman in jogging clothes played fetch with her beagle in the dog run, and a young couple wearing identical knit scarves cuddled at a bench on the opposite end of the park.

From the Facebook photos Gil recognized Amy and Carrie sitting atop a picnic table where they smoked cigarettes and chatted with a third girl. Amy had suggested he email his photo to her, and she waved back when he raised his arm in greeting. Maya's friends moved his way with the third girl trailing behind.

"We thought you could buy us some burgers in exchange for us talking to you," Amy stated when they all stood face to face.

Amy was the ringleader—brash and confident. Carrie and the other girl looked away, but Amy stared at Gil, defiantly waiting for his response.

"I could do that," Gil said. "Is it okay with your parents or whoever? I don't want anyone to think there's anything improper."

"What's improper about going to Five Guys?" Amy asked, with hands on her hips. She was the girl-next-door, blonde type. Outgoing and aware of her good looks.

"Am I taking all three of you for burgers?"

"Yes," Carrie said. "You wanted to ask us about Maya. Well, you can talk to her yourself. This is Maya."

Amy said "sweet" at the sight of Gil's Mustang and immediately hopped into the front passenger seat. Maya sat in the back with Carrie. Gil noticed her glancing at him in the rearview mirror. The girls directed Gil to a strip mall twenty minutes outside of downtown Kalamazoo, an enormous socio-economic distance from their neighborhood.

Situated at a corner table out of earshot of others, they gobbled juicy bacon burgers with mustard, pickles, and onions, and shared three cups of French fries with lots of ketchup. Gil had marveled at the amount of food Jason consumed, but these three suburban teenage girls were formidable competitors. Maya's friends chatted about the two guys behind the counter, their mani-pedi appointments, and some teacher who regularly made passes at the female students. Only a year older than her friends, Maya's countenance was reserved. She nodded at their remarks and agreed the burger boys were cute, but there was a sadness about her as if she had put her teen years far behind her.

After the burgers were eaten and soft drinks slurped down to the ice, Maya's friends excused themselves to visit the accessories store a few doors down. Maya stayed to talk, and share the roasted peanuts—a mainstay at Five Guys.

"I wasn't expecting to see you today. Thank you for agreeing to talk to me."

"Amy said you were cool. She said I could trust you. You work for Jason's parents?"

"Yes. I'm a private investigator."

"A lot of the boys' parents hired investigators. They've been snooping around and asking my friends and neighbors a lot of questions about me. One of the investigators even called my ex-boyfriend."

Maya drew in a deep breath, pursing her lips and staring at the tabletop. She was a very pretty girl, but seemed not to want to show it. There was a hint of a lighter color at the roots of her short hair. Her tired eyes were the color of chestnuts. She wore no makeup, but Gil noticed her nails were painted a deep purple when she tugged at the sleeves of an oversized gray sweater.

"It's not uncommon, as you probably know, to try to make the victim of an assault case look, uh, bad."

"It's not fair," Maya blurted. Her face tightened in anger.

"I agree. My business partner and I told Jason's parents that we're positive you were given some kind of date-rape drug. We made it clear to them that we wouldn't be a party to your character assassination."

Maya grabbed a few peanuts, glancing up at Gil and then back at the table. "Thanks for that."

"Do you mind if I take notes while we talk?"

Maya shook her head.

Gil opened his notebook to a new page and retrieved a pen. "Can you tell me what happened the night of the assault?"

Maya reached up to twirl a strand of her hair, then self-consciously dropped her hands into her lap. She poured a few peanuts onto a napkin.

"You can start anywhere you want," Gil encouraged. "How did you know about the fraternity party?"

"I got an invite and I didn't want to go alone, so I asked Amy and Carrie. They were excited to be going to a college party. They told their folks they were hanging out with me and would stay overnight at my dorm. We got to the party around eleven. There were a lot of people there, guys and girls. And really good music. I was drinking a lot. Too much. Everybody was drinking. It's the thing to do. Some people were also smoking weed. I think there were some guys doing lines, but in another room. I don't do the drug thing; neither do Carrie and Amy. But we had a lot to drink."

"Did anyone hand you a drink?"

"No. Not really. Several times I scooped some of the punch they were serving. It was spiked. With gin I think. But people were passing beers and wine coolers."

"Do you remember anyone in particular bringing you a drink?"

"I think Faith gave me a wine cooler. She's the one who invited me to the party."

"Faith," Gil said scribbling in his notebook. "What's her last name?"

"Victor. She's a freshman."

Gil jotted the additional information. Maya was staring at his notebook when he looked up. He smiled.

"So you, Amy, and Carrie were drinking, but not using any of the drugs at the party. What happened after that?"

"At about one-thirty, some of the girls started to leave, so I told Amy and Carrie we should go, but they were talking with a couple of guys and wanted to stay."

"Was Faith still at the party?"

"Yes. I think so. Her boyfriend is one of the Gamma guys."

Gil scribbled a note.

"We were all sitting on the couch. I got up to get another cup of punch, and a guy at the table offered to pour it for me. That's when I think I got drugged. I know I started to feel horrible. The room was spinning, and I told Amy I was going to be sick."

"Did either Amy or Carrie get a bad drink?"

"I don't know. Maybe not. They were drinking wine coolers. They said they fell asleep."

"Do you remember being taken upstairs?"

"Not really. I remember somebody trying to help me to the bathroom because I was going to be sick. I think I passed out. The next thing I was aware of was when this guy was on top of me. But . . . I couldn't move."

Maya dropped the peanuts. She pulled the neck of her sweater over her face and cried quietly. Gil wanted to reach across the table to touch her elbow, but thought better of it. He turned a page in his book and doodled. After a few minutes, Maya reached for her drink, slurping air and melted ice through the straw.

"You want another?"

Maya nodded.

Gil ordered two more Cokes. When he returned to the table he noticed Maya's eyes and face were red. They sat quietly for a while.

"Maya, I'm very sorry about what happened to you."

She wasn't in the mood for any more sympathy or tears. She sat upright and entwined her hands on the table.

"I don't remember a lot of what happened that night. I can't even remember how I got home. All you *really* care about is finding out if Jason was one of the boys who raped me. I don't know, okay?" Maya's voice was angry. She stared at Gil, her eyes challenging.

Gil said softly, "I *do* hope I can prove Jason wasn't one of your attackers. That's the job I'm being paid for, but I do care. My partner, Charlene Mack, and I both care about what happens to you."

Gil let his words sink in. He hoped she believed him. He watched her draw on her straw, then look at her phone. With the grand jury case less than two weeks away, the pressure on Maya and her family—from lawyers, police, prosecutors, and investigators—must be mounting.

"Do you have any more questions?" she asked, finally looking up.

"Did you know Jason before the party?"

"Not really. He's in one of my classes."

"Which one?"

"Psychology 101."

"Do you like that class?"

"It's okay. The teacher uses TV and movie clips, so it makes it more interesting than some of the other electives."

"Did you know any of the other boys before you went to the party?"

"I'd seen some of the Gamma guys around. They're a party fraternity and their members know a lot of people. Some of the Greeks only hang out with their own kind. You know, like the business majors hang together and the sports guys like to party with their teammates, but the Gammas had people from all those groups at their house parties."

"I just have one more thing, Maya. I've been told there's a video of your assault that's on a site called Flickr."

"I heard about it," she said sorrowfully.

"You haven't seen it?"

"No. But I think Carrie has."

"I'd like to ask Carrie about it. Can we go talk to her?"

Gil and Maya walked along the sidewalk of the strip mall to the accessories store. In the window display there were cutout stars and unicorn decals along the border, and half-mannequins wore bracelets, scarves, and boas. It was the kind of place where young women and teen girls could spend hours posing in the mirrors with gold hoops held up to their ears, or checking out the look of a belt or a sequined cap. Gil hesitated outside the shop.

"Uh, I don't think I belong in there. I'll wait for you in the car, and then drive you guys back to your neighborhood."

"Oh, you don't have to wait for us. We can take the bus home."

"But I need to speak to Carrie before I leave."

"Oh, I forgot. Okay, I'll get her for you."

Maya stepped into the store and moments later Carrie dashed out of the door with a distracted look, already eager to return to her friends and her shopping. Her eyes darted around and finally landed on Gil.

"You want to ask me something?"

"Maya says maybe you saw the video of the rape at the fraternity house."

At the word "rape," Carrie's shopping excitement drained from her face. She stuck her hands in her pockets and scraped the toe of her boot on the sidewalk. Gil hadn't noticed that Carrie was kind of a chubby girl, not quite as pretty as Maya and Amy, but trying hard to keep up. She wore too much eye shadow, and her teeth were a bit too white.

"I saw it. On somebody's phone."

"Could you get me a copy of it?"

"You can get it yourself. It's online."

Gil gave Carrie a clueless look. "Online?"

"On the internet."

"Could you show me how?" Gil handed his phone to Carrie.

"Any passcode?" she asked.

"Nope."

"You should get a passcode."

She pushed buttons until she found what she wanted.

"You have to join Flickr. What username and password do you want?"

Frustrated, Gil thought a minute. "How about 'SlickGil' for the name, and 'all-city' for the password."

"The password has to be at least eight characters, and have at least one numeral."

"Okay, use GA5435773."

"What's that?" Carrie asked punching keys.

"My dog tag number."

This time Carrie showed the clueless gaze.

"Like the number you get when you're in the military? I was a marine."

"Got it. My older brother is in the military. Army. He's in Iraq." She looked back at the screen. "Okay. Now you're a member of the Flickr community." Carrie held out the phone for Gil to see. "Just use the search function, and type in Gamma Fun."

"Wow. You're good. Where's the search function?"

"Right there," Carrie said, pointing.

Gil fumbled with the phone, carefully poking at the keyboard.

"It goes faster if you use your thumbs."

"My thumbs are too big."

"You should get an Apple phone. It has a touch screen. Easier to use."

"I'll tell our office manager."

Gil found the page, and several videos were listed. He held the phone toward Carrie.

"Which one is it?"

"I've only seen one, but I hear there are two, maybe three recordings."

Gil and Carrie shared a somber look. Gil pushed the play icon on one of the videos. It was different from the one Detective Holt had emailed. The quality was a bit better, and it showed a different angle of the bedroom. Carrie slid her hands under her armpits as she hugged herself. She stared at the sidewalk and did the toe thing again.

"Don't let Maya look at these," Gil said when he closed his phone.

Carrie shook her head.

"By the way, were you the one who told the police where they could find these videos?"

Carrie squinted at Gil. "Thanks for the food," she said, turning and going back into the store.

"Wanna get some lunch?" Don peeked up at Charlie from his paperwork.

"I have to get these checks signed for Judy, and I have four more calls to return."

Disappointment crossed, then swiftly disappeared, from Don's face. He grabbed his revolver from the top drawer, and stood to secure it in his shoulder holster.

"Where are you eating?" asked Charlie.

"I'll probably just go to the deli. I can bring something back. You want a Reuben?"

"You know, on second thought, I'll come with you."

Charlie and Don crossed State Street and walked against a steady stream of pedestrians heading south toward Cobo and city hall. The deli was housed in a narrow storefront wedged between two office buildings. There were counter diners and people eating at a half-dozen small tables, competing for space with those edging forward in a serpentine takeout line. Don and Charlie stepped around the queue hoping to find seats, and saw two at the farthest end of the counter, but separated by a lone male diner.

"Excuse me?" Charlie smiled at seventy-five watts to a middle-aged white businessman. He was hunched over a burger and a plate of fries. He glanced up with sandwich-bulging cheeks and a look of suspicion. "Would it be too presumptuous of me to ask if you might move to the other seat, so my friend and I could sit together?"

Don hovered behind Charlie, looking over her shoulder and not smiling. He and his demographic cohort made quick eye contact. The man didn't even reply, just shoved his plate and drink over and, with a bounce, shifted from one stool to the other.

"Thank you."

The man grunted.

Charlie and Don grabbed menus, scanned them for the daily specials, and quickly returned them to the slot in the metal condiments rack.

"What's up?" Charlie asked. "You seem distracted, and more surly than usual."

Don snatched a few napkins from the dispenser just to have something to do, then blurted: "Rita's pregnant."

The man with the burger glanced at them quickly, then down at his plate.

"Congratulations," Charlie said in a lowered voice. "It's time Rudy had a little brother or sister. Right?"

Don didn't respond. Charlie waited. She watched the waitress fill water glasses and top off coffee cups before making her way to their end of the counter. They ordered, and the waitress returned with glasses of water and Vernors. Don sucked half the ginger ale through his straw before talking.

"Things are not all that simple, Mack. Because Rudy is on the autism spectrum, there's a chance the baby will be, too." Don leaned on his elbows and looked at Charlie. "Rita is good with everything. She never worries. But I'm scared stiff."

"Is there some kind of test you can do?" Charlie asked.

"There's no prenatal test to determine autism, and Rita wouldn't stand for it even if there was one."

"What are you going to do?"

"We go to see a specialist next week."

"Do you know the baby's sex?"

"Rita doesn't want to know that either."

The food arrived, and they made small talk. Charlie provided colorful descriptions of the other jurors and the prosecutors. Don asked about some of the specifics of the trial, and to keep his mind off his worries Charlie offered a few details.

"You'd think with the attention the FBI is giving Detroit right now, everybody would know to bury the evidence," Don said.

"These aren't recent charges. Canova allegedly offered these bribes in 2005."

"Rumors have swirled about that guy for twenty years. He cracks the law, but doesn't quite break it. Sounds like he's not sparing any expense on his defense."

"Nope." Charlie grabbed a pinch of runaway sauerkraut and stuffed it back into her Reuben. "And having a celebrity attorney has not been a waste of his money. Bateman's handling himself well."

They left the claustrophobic diner and Charlie took a deep

breath. Clouds kept the temperatures near fifty degrees, but the day was pleasant. They took a detour to Hart Plaza to stay outdoors a while longer and walk off lunch. When they stepped into the elevator of their office building, Charlie touched Don's arm.

"For what it's worth, I believe everything will work out with the new baby."

"Thanks, Mack. It's good to have someone I can talk to."

Gil arrived at the office at three-thirty. Charlie settled into the chair she normally occupied in their conference room. It wasn't at the head of the table, but nearest the whiteboard so she could use the colored Post-it notes that helped her visualize the questions, facts, and assumptions of a case. It was a low-tech method, but had the combination of the tactile and Socratic elements she found effective for her problem-solving. Charlie was rarely more comfortable than in this room, with this group of colleagues. They were her extended family.

"Whaddya got, Gil?" Charlie asked.

"Things are looking up. I met with Maya Hebert today."

"The girl who was raped?" Judy asked.

"That's right. Maya's girlfriends, Amy and Carrie, brought her along to our meeting. She gave me her side of the story."

"That's excellent," Charlie said. "I hadn't been able to reach her."

"She's purposely stayed out of sight. For a while she was hounded by the press, and she and her family have been harassed. Her parents added security cameras to their house after Maya received death threats."

"That's messed up," Don said.

"Maya understands we're working for Jason, but she also seemed to believe me when I told her we aren't the ones who want to hurt her."

"What's she like?" Judy asked.

"A nice young lady. Sad. She was very forthcoming. She admits she and her friends had too much to drink, and she believes a date-rape drug was put in the punch she drank at the party. She really has no recollection of being carried upstairs. All she remembers is feeling woozy, and then waking up as she was being raped. She couldn't even move."

"How can people do such things?" Judy asked. "That's just sick."

"I agree," Gil said.

"These assaults are becoming too common," Charlie said. "I can think of a half-dozen I've heard about this year."

"Maya is courageous to put herself through the prying and threats and the sideways stares she must be getting," Gil said. "But by speaking up, she's really made a difference in the way her university responds to sexual assaults. That's a positive."

"I'm glad there's something positive in all this," Judy said dourly.

"What did Maya have to say about Jason?" Charlie asked.

"They had a class together, but she didn't really know him before the party. I don't think she knew anyone from the fraternity very well. She doesn't know if Jason participated in the assault or not. She just can't remember."

"Who invited her to the party?"

"It was a girlfriend of one of the Gamma boys. I have her name, and I'll check her out."

"I'm really sorry this happened to her," Charlie said.

"I said exactly that to her."

"Anything else?"

"Yes. Something helpful. I told you the police were aware of videos of the assault?"

Charlie nodded. "The lady cop told you."

"Right. And she sent me a link to one of them. But now I have a second one."

"Good work, Romeo," Charlie said.

"It's nothing like that. Maya's friend, Carrie, showed me how to get it from the internet. She downloaded it to my phone."

"Damn, you can do that?" Don asked.

Gil began pressing his phone keyboard.

"Wait," Judy said. "Let's just put it on the monitor."

"You can do *that*?" Gil asked.

"Sure."

Charlie, Don and Gil watched in awe. Judy was the oldest person in the agency and managed the office filing system like a 1950s secretary. Everything was a hard copy with a backup— color-coded and cross-referenced—but with teenagers at home she had the best knowledge of new communications technology. She'd programmed all their ring tones, set up the conference room for video meetings, and showed the Mack partners how to sync their digital cameras to their laptops. She turned on the conference room laptop and connected it to the TV monitor.

"What website has the video? YouTube?"

"No. It's called Flickr."

"Oh, that's right." Judy began typing into the laptop. "I have it." She turned the laptop toward Gil. "Here, put in your user name and password."

Gil punched in the info and pushed the laptop to Judy.

"What's the name of the file?" she asked, moving her cursor.

"Unfortunately, it's called Gamma Fun."

They watched the forty-inch monitor as Judy scrolled through a list of files.

"That's the one," Gil said. "Gamma Fun by Xtopher."

The two-minute video was dim, shot from a distance, but it clearly showed a rumpled bed in a small room, and a girl being sexually attacked. The walls of the room were lined with onlookers—young men and women. Thankfully, there was no sound on the video, but you could see some of the people laughing, their faces contorted in excitement. The person taking the video shakily zoomed in to the bed, and Maya's horrified face was clear for a moment, as a boy on top of her held her arms down.

"Damn," Don said when the video ended.

The others sat in stunned silence.

"Do you want to see it again?" Judy finally asked.

"No." Charlie spoke for everyone. "No, we don't. Judy, is there a way to make a copy of the footage?"

"Yes. I'll figure it out."

"Do you think I should show it to the Ferrys?" Gil asked Charlie.

"I don't think so. But if the video somehow disappears from this site, I want us to have a copy. Jason may be guilty of witnessing the assault and not doing anything to help Maya, but so are a lot of other people in that room. At some point, Jason's lawyer may want him to identify the others on the video."

"I don't think he'll want to do that," Gil said.

"He may not have a choice if he wants to stay out of jail."

Judy requested a fifteen-minute break. She was shaken by the video and wanted to call her kids—two teenaged boys, and a preteen girl. Don used the time to return a phone call to one of the subcontractors. Charlie and Gil remained at the conference table.

"That video is tough to watch."

"According to Carrie, Maya hasn't seen any of the footage. I hope her parents haven't either."

"You liked her?"

"I really did. And her friends. Teenaged girls are a whole special kind of human being." Gil chuckled. "One moment they were thoughtful and sensitive, the next giggling about the boys at the restaurant. Carrie taught an old guy like me how to use his own phone. I could tell she was angry and disturbed about the videos, but then she was off to buy headbands and get her nails polished. It was quite head-spinning, but they all seem very resilient."

"Even Maya?"

"I think she'll be all right. She's an intelligent girl. She's still dealing with the pain of what's happened to her. She's cautious about who to trust, and I don't blame her. Maya strikes me as someone who will use this horrible event to become a stronger person. She doesn't want to be seen as a victim."

"Between Jason, and now Maya and her friends, you're spending a lot of time with young people."

"You're telling me. Before the other day, I hadn't set foot inside a high school in a dozen years. It was an experience."

"Count it as research. You'll be having some kids of your own one of these days."

"Yeah. Maybe," Gil said, blushing.

"What? Is something going on with Darla? Are you guys talking about having kids?"

"No. No. Nothing like that. But I am thinking about popping the question."

"Well, what do you know," Charlie said, beaming. "My brother-from-another-mother is getting married."

"Wait a minute. You're jumping the gun, Charlie."

"What's this about a gun?" Don asked, returning to the conference room.

Gil shushed Charlie with a look.

"Nothing."

When Judy rejoined them at the table, it was time for Charlie to present the issue that had been on her mind since yesterday.

"I need help with something. There's this guy who's been at the courthouse. I know I've seen him before, but I just can't place him." Charlie activated her phone and passed it to Judy.

"More phone pictures?" Judy asked as she peered at the screen, then shook her head. "I don't know who that is." Judy passed the instrument to Don who squinted at the screen.

"Casper?"

"Who?" Gil asked, reaching out for the phone.

"I think that's his name. Casper, from somewhere in New Jersey. Maybe Trenton. He was involved in a money-laundering case we had at DHS."

"How do you remember that?" Judy asked.

"I'm not just a pretty face, Novak."

"You're not a pretty face at all," Judy retorted.

Don ignored the insult with a sneer. "As I recall, we questioned a bunch of people in that case, but we never talked to him."

Charlie stared at the screen again. "That doesn't ring any bells, but I knew he looked familiar. Yesterday was the second time I'd seen him around the courthouse."

"Wait a minute," Gil said. "Let me see that photo again." Gil stared, adjusting the screen and switching between the longer view Charlie had taken, and the close-up. "I *do* remember this guy, Don. We didn't question him because we couldn't find him. Remember? He fell off the radar. That's why we started calling him the ghost. Like Casper the ghost."

Charlie finally remembered the man with the unique nickname. She agreed to call one of their contacts at Homeland Security to get more information on this elusive criminal.

"Charlene Mack. To what, or whom, do I owe the honor of this call?"

"Casper, the ghost."

"What?" Tony Canterra asked.

"A guy who was in the mix in a money laundering case we looked at after 9/11. Don remembered his name is Casper. Not sure if that's a first or surname. We were following a tip about how the terrorists got access to the cash they used for the airplane attacks. We think this guy might have been based in New Jersey."

"So, that was five years ago. What's your interest now?"

"I think I've seen the guy recently."

"Oh yeah? Where?"

"Here in Detroit. Near the courthouses. I'm serving on jury duty."

"Wow. Jury duty. Other than that, how are you?"

"Good."

"How's Mandy Porter?"

"She's good too. And you? How's your life since I saw you last?"

"I'm engaged."

"I bet she's a knockout."

"She is."

"That's wonderful, Tony."

There was a brief pause. Charlie didn't want this conversation to become more personal. She needed to be friendly enough to keep the lines of communication open between the Mack agency and DHS, but she had no interest in revisiting stickier personal issues with Tony.

"I hope you're as happy as I am," Charlie finally said. There was another span of silence before she added: "You think you could send me what you have on this guy?"

"Sure, Charlie. Is that all you need?"

"That's all I need, my friend."

"Okay. I'll have someone pull it together, and get it to you tomorrow."

"That's great, Tony. Thank you. And I'm glad you're happy."

Charlie disconnected the call and folded her arms on the desk. Don stared at her from across the room.

"Canterra still trying to hit on you?"

Charlie leaned back in her chair. "Not really. He's engaged."

"So I heard. A woman with a young kid. Divorced, from his hometown. She moved in with him a few months ago."

"Wow. I see your DHS pipeline is still open."

"It's a small community. He gonna give us the info on the ghost?"

"Yeah. We'll have it tomorrow."

Chapter 7

Friday

Activity at the courthouse on Friday morning moved at a snail's pace. The clerk came in the jury room a few times to take a count as jurors straggled in the door. Today they would hear the testimony of live witnesses. As many as eight, according to the clerk. Charlie watched a few jurors huddle near the windows. The flirtatious Mr. Fletcher saw her looking and left the group to join her at one of the work tables.

"How was your day off?"

"Good. It was nice to sleep in," Charlie lied.

"It certainly was. But I came downtown to the MGM Resort last night. You like to gamble?"

"Do I wear it on my face?" Charlie laughed.

"No. But you seem like a sophisticated lady."

"I've been spending more time doing house projects than gambling lately. That's what's saved me from myself."

"House projects can get expensive. What kind of work are you doing?"

Charlie described the plans she and Mandy had to gut their kitchen, and the work they'd already started with new lighting and sprucing up the bathrooms.

"It all adds up," Fletcher said, staring quizzically.

"Yeah, but what do they say about the casinos?" Charlie

quipped. "The house always has the advantage. At least now the house is mine."

They chuckled, and chatted about their casino experiences until the jury foreman announced it was time to begin their work. The clerk stood at the door checking the roster as they lined up to enter the courtroom. She scowled at the latecomers. "We have a lot of witnesses today. Because we're starting late, we'll probably have shorter breaks. That's the reason it's so important to be on time," she chided.

Spivak and Gleason were efficient and managed to get in five witnesses before the late lunch break. The first witness was Canova's young office assistant, Kendra Vaile, who answered questions about the huge sums of cash a parking company can accrue in a day. She corroborated the accountant's testimony that she walked to the bank—sometimes accompanied by a guard— to make large cash deposits. She also testified that Canova held a large amount of cash in his office safe.

"How much money is usually kept in the safe?" Gleason asked the witness.

"I know I've given Mr. Canova ten thousand dollars for the safe."

"How often does Mr. Canova add cash to the safe, Ms. Vaile?"

"Two or three times a week."

"Is it always ten thousand dollars?"

"No. Usually it's three to five thousand dollars."

"Did Mr. Canova ever tell you why he keeps so much cash in the office?"

"No."

"Who has the combination to access the safe?"

"Well, it used to be Mr. Canova and Harvey."

"And who is Harvey?"

"The accountant, Harvey Rush. Now only Mr. Canova has the combination."

"Thank you, Ms. Vaile. I have no other questions."

The judge looked at the defense table. "Cross, Mr. Bateman?"

"Yes, just a couple of questions, Your Honor." Bateman referred to his legal pad for several seconds. "Ms. Vaile, isn't it true that Mr. Canova sometimes uses cash to pay for things like office parties, employee birthday gifts, and lunches for staff?"

"Yes. He does that all the time."

"Did Mr. Canova ever ask you to hide any of the cash that came across your desk from either Mr. Rush, or the auditor?"

"No. He never asked me to hide any money, and I wouldn't do that even if he did ask me," Vaile said indignantly.

"Of course you wouldn't. No further questions."

"Redirect?" Judge Smoot tossed her question at the prosecutors.

"Yes, Your Honor." Gleason stood. "Ms. Vaile, when there is an office party or a staff lunch, are you the person who organizes those events?"

"Yes. Sometimes I get help from one of the managers, but it's mostly me."

"How much do you normally spend on these events?"

"It varies. Office parties might run a couple of thousand dollars, since all the facility managers and parking attendants are invited."

"How often do you have office parties?"

"Only once or twice a year. At Christmas, and sometimes we do a summer picnic."

"What about the employee birthday gifts, and staff lunches? Do you spend thousands on those things?"

"Oh no. I spend maybe fifty dollars for a gift card or something like that for birthdays. The staff lunches are just for those in the office, they don't cost much."

"And, just to be clear, you said you would prepare cash packets of three thousand dollars for Mr. Canova's safe, two or three times a week?"

"Right. Sometimes more than that."

"Your Honor, I have no more questions for Ms. Vaile."

Another prosecution witness was the Fleetstar parking facility manager who testified about the voluminous amounts of cash that passed hands at his downtown parking garage. Bateman questioned the company's seven year employee about cash management procedures, and surfaced testimony that several Fleetstar employees had been terminated for mishandling or stealing cash.

The last two witnesses of the morning were procurement specialists with the city's licensing department. Each one described the standard procedures of contract bidding, candidate vetting and selection, and the regulations in place to assure a fair process. Allan Bateman used his cross-exam privilege sparingly with the Canova employees, but his questioning of the city staffers was very aggressive. He was adept at creating doubt within the jury about the consistency of Detroit's government procurement rules. By Charlie's gauge, the morning had been a tie between the prosecution and the defense.

The ghost man, Casper whatever his name was, had not appeared in court for the morning session, so Charlie retrieved her cell phone at the lunch break to call the office. When she turned on the phone, it beeped with a voice message from Don. *Call in when you can. You're going to love what we found out about Casper the not-so-friendly ghost.* With a shortened lunch period, she'd have to combine lunch and business. Charlie grabbed her coat and backpack, and sat outside on a low ledge at the side of the courthouse. Judy picked up on the first ring and put Charlie on speaker.

"A courier dropped off an eight-page DHS dossier," Don said. "Your mystery guy has been one step away from incarceration for the last ten years."

"What are the highlights?" Charlie asked, pouring coffee into her thermos top.

"His full name is Caspar Goulet; that's spelled *C-A-S-P-A-R*— not like the ghost. He's originally from Newark. He served time in a New Jersey state prison for armed robbery, then became an associate to one of the Italian mob families in Jersey for a couple of decades. After that he moved to the Tampa area in the late '90s. Like I remembered, he was under suspicion in a money laundering racket connected to a couple of the 9/11 terrorists. His name came up when DHS investigated the flying schools where the terrorists were trained. We couldn't locate him, because by that time he was serving time at a Florida correctional facility under another name and later dropped off the radar," Don finished.

"Hmm. I guess I saw his photo at DHS," Charlie said, sticking a plastic fork into the salad she'd brought for lunch.

"Nope. That's not it," Judy said.

"What do you mean?"

"You've seen the guy more recently than that."

"When?"

"During the Abrams case."

"Stop with the cat-and-mouse, Novak," Don's voice bellowed through the speaker.

"Okay, okay. *You* tell me, Don," Charlie ordered.

"You remember Owens?"

"Owen Owens? Who could forget him?" Charlie said of the sleazy criminal whose actions had put her in peril two years ago.

"Well, Goulet was one of Owens's associates in the human trafficking scheme. We all saw him at the arraignment. He was one of the men who ran the illegal boarding house crammed with all those undocumented workers."

"Exactly!" Charlie shouted. "*That's* why his mug stuck out for me. Shouldn't he be in prison?"

"He should be. Judy did a database search. He had a bunch of charges thrown at him connected to the trafficking, and also the money laundering. Somehow, he was released on bail. He's been on the loose ever since."

"So, does DHS want him?"

"They don't seem to, but I bet the FBI does," Don said. "There's sure to be an outstanding warrant on him. Should I call them?"

"No. Not yet."

"Why not, Mack?"

"Well for one thing, he wasn't even in the courtroom today."

"What's the other thing?"

"I'd like to find out what he's up to before we call in the cavalry," Charlie said. "Judy, where's Gil?"

"He went to meet the Ferrys at their house."

"Can you both stay an extra hour or so tonight?"

"Sure," Don said.

"I can too," Judy agreed.

"Okay. Let Gil know, when you hear from him. I'll see you tonight."

The Mack partners were fifteen minutes into their impromptu brainstorming session and making short work of a basket of assorted chip packets and soft drinks. Don used the whiteboard to make an investigation diagram. In the center was a blowup of Charlie's photo of Caspar Goulet. It was taped alongside a prison photo provided by DHS. Don had used a marker to draw spokes connecting the photos to a New Jersey organized crime syndicate; an evidence-tampering charge in Venice, Florida; the local trafficking case; and the sighting at the Canova trial. Under the heading *Homeland Security* was a bulleted list of details received from the agency.

"What do you think he's after?" Gil asked.

"Probably working for that scumbag, Canova," Don said.

"That seems likely since they share ties to organized crime," Charlie agreed.

"He really looks different in those two photos," Judy noted.

"But you can still tell it's him," Don offered. "Maybe the FBI has an updated photo."

Charlie grabbed three packets of sticky notes and moved to the whiteboard. She peeled off two green notes and quickly wrote the questions: *Why is the ghost interested in the Canova trial? Who was the man he was talking to last week in the corridor?* She placed the notes on the board.

"I don't really see how we go about answering those questions unless we can observe his comings and goings," Don said.

Gil stared at the board. "Has there been a pattern to his showing up at the trial?"

Charlie returned to her seat. She absentmindedly picked up a bag of Cheetos and started munching.

"Well, let's see. I've seen Caspar, with a *p-a-r*, the ghost three times now. He was in the courtroom the first day of the trial.

That's when I also saw him in the corridor, but he wasn't there the whole day."

"Who were the witnesses that day?"

"The bodyguard-slash-chauffeur who had cut a deal with the prosecution."

"When did you see him next?"

"Wednesday. That's when we stayed late to hear the testimony of Canova's accountant."

"He wasn't in the courtroom at all on Tuesday?" Gil asked.

"I don't think so. We had police witnesses that day. And he didn't show up today either when we heard testimony from the city employees."

"Do you usually know in advance what witnesses you'll hear?" Don asked.

Charlie shook her head. "No. But Monday is the beginning of the second week of the trial so the prosecution should, hopefully, be winding down their case, and the defense will present their witnesses."

"What does this Caspar guy do when he's in the courtroom?" Gil asked.

"When the accountant was testifying, I thought he might be taking notes."

"Blending in?" Don asked.

"Could be. He always seems to be checking out the people in the room—like I am. We made eye contact a couple of times. When I saw him in the car across the street from the courthouse, he was just sitting there. He had the window rolled down, and he wore sunglasses."

"He doesn't have on sunglasses in your photo," Judy noted.

"That's right. I forgot. He put on the sunglasses when I looked his way. That's what made me suspicious. When I doubled back and sneaked up on him from the rear, the sunglasses were gone again."

"I have another question to add to the board," Gil said. "If you recognize him, does he recognize you?"

"I'll add that." Charlie scribbled and affixed the green Post-it to the whiteboard.

"I doubt he'd remember you from the Owens arraignment," Don said. "The courtroom was packed. There was a lot of press, police, other defendants, and a bunch of other people."

"Right," Charlie acknowledged.

"But for sure he's noticed you in the jury box."

"I know he has."

"If you see him again, can you contact one of us?" Gil asked, then added, "But you can't have your phone inside the courthouse, can you?"

"No. I'd have to alert you during a break. Then one of you could come over."

"That may not work if he comes and goes," Don said. "He might be gone by the time one of us gets to the courthouse."

"That's true, but it doesn't make sense for you or Gil to sit in the courtroom all day. We have casework to do."

"*I* could do it," Judy said tentatively.

Three pairs of eyes landed on her smile.

"Nobody knows me from Adam. Tamela's doing a fine job in the office, and I'd find it interesting to listen to a trial."

Charlie waited for Don or Gil to object. They didn't. Now Judy's face was one big eager question mark.

"I guess I could signal you from the jury box if he comes into the courtroom," Charlie considered.

"You could. And I've seen the ghost's picture, so I know who to look for," Judy said, getting into the shorthand.

"Then what?" Don asked.

"Well, let's talk about it," Charlie began. "When I signal Judy, she can leave the courthouse and immediately call you, Don. Then you can come over and keep an eye on him. See who he talks to, check out what car he drives, maybe even follow him. What do you think?"

"What's the objective, Charlie?" Gil asked. "Why not just notify DHS or the FBI that we've seen Caspar and let them handle it?"

"That's a good question, Mack." Don leaned back, lacing his fingers behind his head.

"I want to know what he's up to?"

"As a juror, you can't do your own investigation of the case you're hearing," Gil said, wearing his lawyer hat.

"This isn't an investigation of the case. We'll be getting information on a known fugitive."

"How do we know his presence in the courtroom isn't related to the case?" Gil argued.

"Acosta's right, Mack. This Goulet isn't the kind of man who just sits in on trials. He's on somebody's payroll."

"So, whose payroll?" Charlie asked.

"Like I said. Canova," Don growled.

"Could be," Gil said. "Or maybe he's keeping an eye on the trial to make sure Canova doesn't say the wrong thing. He could even be working for one of Canova's enemies."

"You think Canova's being set up for a hit?" Don asked.

"It's a possibility," Gil said.

"That's the point, we just don't know," Charlie said. "So, we need to find out what the ghost is really up to."

The rest of the Mack Team gave Charlie looks ranging from dubious to disagreement.

"You're suggesting we invest quite a bit of time on something we're not getting paid for," Don said.

"We've done that before," Judy reminded them.

"Yes, but for friends or family," Don argued.

"So, I'll ask again," Gil said. "What's our objective?"

"We're doing a favor for a friend. Me."

Charlie's levity hadn't worked. Three stern faces stared back at her. She pointed to the board.

"Aww, come on, guys. Aren't you just a little bit curious to know what he's up to? Let's just see what happens next week. What do you say?"

Chapter 8

Monday

Within ten minutes of tasting the sweet, spiked punch Maya felt her stomach lurch and her head swim. The music seemed, at once, louder and harder to hear. Her face spasmed as if the pounding bass was connected to her muscles. She rose from the couch on rubbery legs, leaning hard against the armrest to steady herself. "I'm okay," she said in response to her friend's query. Not sure why she lied.

She took a few shaky steps toward the archway separating the living room from the dining room. The music was louder here. She eyed the punchbowl on the card table, and the legs of a lanky boy who lingered there. She couldn't quite lift her eyes to assess his guilt, but the toes of his shoes pointed at her in a wide stance. "I feel sick," she thought she said, but was not sure if the call for help escaped her lips. She reached out for the wall beside her and grasped at its coolness, willing her legs to move toward the bathroom. She saw the outline of the open door, light spilling onto the floor, and she could smell the faint odor of urine. She slumped to her knees; the room now spinning out of control, feeling strong hands lifting her, guiding her.

The blackness was very deep. Her eyelids jerked open in panic. The music was distant, muddled with odd chants and the grunts of wild boars. She stared at a white space. Gray around the edges. Then a human face, contorted. It disappeared. Then returned. Different eyes— mouth open. She became aware of pressure against her back. Her torso

70

being lifted. Strong hands gripping her arms. Helping her? Maya heard shouting and laughter. No, not laughing, hooting. She began to run, but couldn't feel her legs move. Her knees were forced apart. A searing pain dashed up her spine. Another face, this one with teeth clenched. The pressure came from front and back now. The white space roiled so she closed her eyes. Tightened her fists. Screamed.

Charlie shouted and jerked back on her pillow. She looked at her legs that were weighted down by Hamm, then turned her head and met Mandy's gaze.

"Bad dream?"

"Yes. But not mine."

Charlie pushed up to lean against the headboard. When she did, Hamm jumped from the bed. She reached for the glass of water on the bed stand.

"It's that Ferry case. Gil spoke to the rape victim last week. I guess she got into my head."

"It feels like you're getting too personally involved in both these trial cases, Charlie. Don't forget what the therapist said about developing a mechanism to help you separate the work you do from who you are."

"Easier said than done."

"That's why people get paid to help with the hard, emotional stuff," Mandy said, kissing Charlie on the cheek. "Okay, I'm on doggie patrol for another week, so I'm going to put Hamm out. Happy Monday. It's another great day for jury duty."

Charlie arrived at the courthouse early, secured her phone and laptop in a locker, and moved to the bank of elevators. Waiting and jockeying for position were courthouse staff, jurors, police officers, and attorneys. Charlie remembered the stairwell and walked up the two flights. As she stepped into the corridor, she spotted Goulet at a bench chatting with the man she'd seen him with the week before. Based on his briefcase and appearance, Goulet's companion was probably an attorney. The two men didn't look her way, and Charlie quickly moved in the opposite direction toward Courtroom Five, but before entering the hallway for the jury room, she sat at a bench and pulled out her thermos. Pretending to drink, she peered over the cup for a better look at the ghost's companion. The young African-American man wore designer glasses. His patterned socks peeked between the pants of a well-cut suit and tan dress shoes. His neatly trimmed beard merged into a fresh haircut. He was definitely an attorney, albeit a young, well-dressed one.

Charlie contemplated returning to her locker for her phone to alert Don that the ghost was on-site, but then the elevator doors opened, and a dozen people exited. The two men glanced up from their conversation and moved further down the corridor away from the elevators. Charlie watched the fashion juror step out, hesitate, and stare at the backs of Goulet and the lawyer before turning toward the jury room. Charlie quickly recapped her thermos and hurried into the hallway. She nodded to a few of the other jurors and turned to greet the young woman as she entered behind her.

"How are you doing this morning?" Charlie asked. "You look fabulous as always."

"Thank you. I'm so tired today. I can't wait for this trial to be over. I've got things to do with my life besides being here." She pouted.

"I know what you mean."

The morning session continued the testimony introduced on Friday—explaining the boring intricacies of government procurement. Charlie's head swam with the jargon of contracting: RFPs, purchasing protocols, indemnifications, bidding rules, awards cycles, option years, and waiver of subrogation. Next to her Richard Fletcher snored softly, and the fashionista had begun a quick repair to her nails with a file. Charlie glanced at the gallery. The ghost hadn't appeared in the courtroom, but Judy sat in the third row, leaning forward, and listening with rapt attention. This bureaucratic gobbledygook was just the kind of nerdy stuff she loved.

Charlie stifled a yawn and peeked at the door as it opened. The

72

ghost stepped into the courtroom and sat in the last row. Charlie shifted in her chair in an attempt to get Judy's attention, but Judy was transfixed by the witness from the city's Department of General Services. It was another ten long minutes before Spivak stopped his questioning and turned toward the defense attorney. Bateman appeared to have just awakened from a nap. With the gratitude of the jury, he conducted a brief cross-examination of the witness.

When the judge announced a twenty-minute break, Judy finally looked up, and Charlie signaled with a slight tilt of her head toward the rear of the courtroom. Judy looked back just as Goulet rose and headed for the exit. She nodded and followed.

When the trial resumed, Goulet returned to the courtroom, but not Judy. The ghost moved to the third row of the gallery, and gave a not-so-quick glance toward the jury box. His eyes connected with Charlie's for only a second. But she sensed her seat mates also staring in his direction. Spivak turned the questioning duties over to his colleague, Karen Gleason, who called one of the key witnesses in the trial, the city manager who the prosecution alleged had taken a bribe from Canova.

Adrienne Raab had not been in the courtroom for the earlier testimony, but now—sitting between two men in the first row of the gallery—she handed her purse to one of them as she walked to the stand. Her other companion had the telltale signs of being an attorney. Raab was a cool customer. Her salt-and-pepper hair was elegantly coifed, and she wore a muted-green pantsuit with brown heels and a tan blouse. She confidently raised her hand to be sworn in.

Gleason took her time moving papers around on the table. She looked up once at Raab, then continued making three piles and squaring them up neatly. Canova attempted eye contact with Raab, but she kept her eyes on the far wall of the courtroom, seeming quite content to wait. Finally, Gleason stood.

"Your Honor, I wish to treat this witness as hostile."

"You may proceed, Ms. Gleason."

Gleason began her questioning with a single sheet of paper in hand. "Would you state your full name?"

"Adrienne L. Raab."

"Where do you live?"

"I live in Detroit."

"Are you married?"

"Yes."

"For whom do you work?"

"I work for the city of Detroit."

"What is your position?"

"I'm a Supervisory Procurement Officer in the Department of General Services."

The questioning went on like that for five minutes with the back-and-forth rhythm of straightforward questions and to-the-point responses. Gleason slowly and deliberately shuffled through papers, and finally substituted the single sheet for a set of documents. Charlie was aware of this slow-pace ploy used by some lawyers to keep a witness anxious, but it wasn't working on Raab. She remained composed, sitting stone still, eyes fixed on the rear of the room.

While everyone waited for Gleason, the door opened noisily and the bailiff, clerk, most of the jury, and a few people in the gallery took note of Don entering. He looked over at Charlie, scanned the courtroom, and took a seat in the row behind Caspar, who seemed preoccupied with the contents of a folder.

"Ms. Raab," Gleason finally said. "Do you know the defendant, Mr. Francis Canova?"

"I've met him."

"Where did you meet Mr. Canova?"

"He manages several city-owned parking facilities. The city hosts a holiday event for our key vendors and contractors. I believe I met him there."

"Have you ever accepted money from Mr. Canova?"

"No."

"I have a series of questions for you about May 19, 2005."

"Okay."

"Where were you on the afternoon of that day?"

"What day of the week was it?"

"Thursday."

"I would have been at work."

"Didn't you leave work sometime during the afternoon?"

"I may have left to get lunch."

"Did you visit Chene Park that afternoon?"

"I might have if the weather was nice. Sometimes I take a lunch and sit near the water."

"This would have been after lunchtime, Ms. Raab. Around 2 p.m. Do you eat lunch that late?"

"Sometimes. Depends on the day."

Gleason stared at Raab a moment, then flipped the page on the legal pad she was using for her questions.

"Approach, Your Honor?"

With the judge's permission, Gleason moved toward the witness box and leaned toward Raab.

"Did you meet Mr. Canova on May 19, 2005, at Chene Park?"

"As I've said. I don't really know Mr. Canova. So, no I didn't meet him that day."

"Have you ever had a phone conversation with Mr. Canova?"

"It's possible we've spoken by phone. I sometimes have to resolve issues with vendors."

"What about emails? Have you communicated with Mr. Canova by email?"

"Possibly."

"What about that day?"

"I don't recall."

"Well let me refresh your memory," Gleason said, whipping out a page from those in her hands, and thrusting it at the witness.

Raab looked at the paper. For the first time, her composure slipped. She lifted her eyes to Gleason's smug face.

Bateman interjected. "Your Honor. What is the exhibit Ms. Gleason is using?"

The judge looked at Gleason, who responded: "Exhibit 24-A.

I may also be using Exhibits 24-B and 24-C with this witness, Your Honor."

Bateman grabbed the huge binder of exhibits on the table, and thumbed through it until he found the documents. He pushed the binder toward Canova and pointed to the item. The two men leaned toward each other and whispered.

"May I continue Your Honor?"

Harrington-Smoot glanced at Bateman. "You may, Ms. Gleason."

"Have you seen this email before?" the prosecutor asked.

"I don't believe so."

"What's the date of the email?"

"May 18, 2005."

"Is it addressed to your business email?"

"Yes."

"And what does the subject line read?"

"Deadline." Raab gave a quick glance toward her companions in the gallery.

"Please read the body of the email, Ms. Raab," Gleason persisted.

"I'm concerned about my license renewal. When is the deadline?" Raab read.

"How is the email signed?"

"FC."

"And from what address did this email originate?"

"Chief at Fleetstar dot com."

"Please read the reply in this email thread, Ms. Raab."

Raab looked directly at Gleason, and without looking at the paper again said: "CP. Tomorrow at 2 p.m."

"Did you send this email?"

"I don't recall."

"What does CP mean?"

"I have no idea."

"Could it mean Chene Park?"

"Like I said, I have no idea what CP means. I don't recall this email."

Gleason moved again to the prosecutor's table and retrieved another document. She made a show of taking a pen and circling several places on the page. The tension in the courtroom was as acute as when Canova's driver had deteriorated to profanity. Charlie shot a glance at the visitors' area. Goulet looked intently at the witness. Don looked intently at Goulet.

Gleason completed her paper theatrics and turned to face the witness.

"Ms. Raab, what is your office phone number?"

"The General Services telephone number is 313-555-0101. My extension is 3105."

"Do you have a mobile number?"

"Yes."

"What is that number?"

Raab hesitated. "I don't feel comfortable providing my private number in open court."

Gleason didn't miss a beat. She asked permission to approach the witness.

"Okay. Would you write your mobile number on this." She walked to the witness box with a slip of note paper.

Raab wrote something on the small square, and returned it to Gleason. The prosecutor smiled, gave the paper to the court reporter, and waited for its return. Gleason placed the hand written note in front of Spivak and retrieved the document she'd marked. Gleason fixed her gaze on the jury as she walked unhurriedly to the witness box and extended the new document. Raab's face went pale.

"Your Honor, this is a portion of exhibit 16-C," Gleason said.

Bateman turned several pages in his exhibit book, pushed it toward Canova, and slumped in his chair.

"Ms. Raab. This is a phone record for Frank Canova's cell phone. Do you recognize the number which I've circled on this sheet?"

Raab glared at the female prosecutor, but didn't answer.

"Ms. Raab. Do you recognize the number circled on Mr. Canova's phone record as the one you just provided to the court clerk?"

Raab stared down at her lap, still not responding.

"Your Honor, would you direct the witness to answer the question?"

Raab lifted her head toward the judge. The magistrate removed her glasses, cleared her throat, and peered down at the witness. "Ms. Raab, you are required to answer the question. Do you need the question repeated?"

Raab shook her head. She folded her arms tightly across her chest. "I refuse to answer that question on the grounds that it may incriminate me."

Gleason's next twenty questions were met with Raab's repetitive invoking of the Fifth Amendment. It became a bizarre and hypnotic dance between prosecutor and witness, each performing their moves as rehearsed.

Raab had regathered her composure. She waited patiently for the prosecutor to jostle papers, move back and forth between the attorney table and witness box, and recite her questions. Raab then spoke the rote reply guaranteed her by the Constitution.

The judge banged her gavel. "Okay, let's take a lunch break. Ms. Raab, we'll see you back here after lunch." The judge looked at the jurors. "Only sixty minutes today, folks. Let's reconvene at one-thirty."

Charlie pretended to adjust her shirt sleeve in her jacket, letting those jurors in her row slide by, so she could side-eye the courtroom. She watched Goulet move quickly to the exit, and acknowledged Don's nod as he trailed. Charlie slowly looped her arms into her backpack straps, and watched Ms. Raab and the men who had accompanied her to court pause in a dejected huddle near the door.

Charlie bypassed the jury room and made a beeline to her phone. She dialed Judy's cell number as she walked away from the courthouse and toward Greektown.

"Hi. Where are you?"

"I came back to the office. You on your lunch break?"

"I am."

"Did Don make it to the courtroom?"

"Yes, and he took off after the ghost."

78

"Great. Charlie, that trial is fascinating."

"You are such a nerd. Even the judge looked like she wanted to fall asleep during that procurement testimony. You missed a bit of drama when the next witness testified."

"Drat! Who was it?"

"The woman from the city who allegedly took a bribe from Canova. I'll tell you all about it when I see you."

"You expect Don back in the courtroom this afternoon?"

"I'm not sure. But in case I don't see him, and you hear from him, tell him I want to meet at the office again tonight. I should be there by 6 p.m."

"What about Gil?"

"Tell him the same thing."

Charlie continued along St. Antoine Street toward the Greektown Casino. There wasn't a lot of green space in the court area of Downtown Detroit. She passed the Wayne County Jail and the Juvenile Detention Facility and veered into the casino where she knew she could find a seat in the food court. She purchased a banana, and found a corner table where she had a view of a bank of slot machines and one of the hallways. She poured coffee from her thermos and retrieved the egg salad sandwich on whole grain bread she'd packed for lunch. She laid everything out on a paper towel and admired the shades of brown and yellow.

Pulling a book from her backpack, she immediately transformed the bells, buzzers, shouts, cash-out coins, music, and *Wheel of Fortune* chants into background noise. She finished a chapter of the book, the sandwich, and took a last swallow of coffee, then checked her watch. She still had twenty minutes. She tried Don on his cell, but he didn't pick up. Charlie had almost finished her banana when she saw someone she recognized walking through the casino floor. Mr. Fletcher, flanked by two other jurors on the Canova trial, didn't look her way as they passed the food court but Charlie instinctively lifted the book to cover her face. She checked her watch again. Only fifteen min utes to get back.

Charlie grabbed her backpack, threw away her lunch trash,

and exited the casino through the valet parking exit. A block away from Frank Murphy Hall of Justice, Charlie saw the three jurors up ahead. They were in the midst of an intense conversation on the sidewalk across from the courthouse. Charlie had heard the woman mention that she worked at Blue Cross Blue Shield. The bearded white guy mainly kept to himself, but he was one of the regular smokers in the courtyard. He shoved a finger against Fletcher's chest a couple of times as he made a point. Fletcher stood his ground and talked back. The Blue Cross lady glanced Charlie's way, spotted her, and said something to the two men. They all stopped talking and turned to look at her. Fletcher threw up a hand in a wave, and Charlie waved back.

The prosecution's examination of Adrienne Raab picked up again. Neither Don nor the ghost had returned to the courtroom, and Charlie adjusted herself in the seat to get ready for the continuation of the Fifth Amendment *pas de deux*. Ten minutes into the questioning, Karen Gleason shifted gears into territory Raab was willing to talk about.

"Ms. Raab, you indicated earlier that you're married."

"That's right."

"How long have you been married?"

"Eighteen years."

"Are you familiar with the Alpine Motel?"

Raab froze. Her face took on a look of total panic. She looked at Gleason, toward her companions in the courtroom, and then toward the judge. Allan Bateman leaned toward Canova, whispering, and the defendant shrugged his shoulders.

"I object, Your Honor. What relevance does this question have to this trial?" Bateman asked.

"Your Honor, I intend to show the relevance very shortly," Gleason said.

"Since you've declared Ms. Raab a hostile witness, I'll give you a bit of leeway, Ms. Gleason, but connect the dots on this very quickly," Judge Harrington-Smoot warned.

Gleason continued. "Have you ever visited the Alpine Motel?"

Raab looked like a trapped animal. Her lips quivered, baring her teeth, and her eyes were wide and unblinking. She clutched the ledge of the witness box with both hands squeezing so tightly her fingers were discolored.

"I . . . I don't know what you mean," Raab stuttered.

"Do you know Kenneth Smith?"

"I . . . I don't know."

"Mr. Smith is the General Manager for Canova Enterprises. Does that improve your recollection?"

Raab fought to regain her professional demeanor. She tried to make eye contact with her friends in the gallery, but they were engaged in a whispered conversation.

"I refuse to answer on the grounds that it might incriminate me."

Allan Bateman stood at his table. "Your Honor, may we approach the bench?"

"I'm going to do you one better, Mr. Bateman," Judge Harrington-Smoot said loudly. "We're taking a fifteen-minute recess. Ladies and gentlemen of the jury, please return to the jury room. Ms. Raab, this is just a break in your testimony. I expect you back. Counselors, you will join me in my chambers." The judge banged the gavel to give emphasis to her orders.

The jury room lit up with gossip. There was not enough time to grab a smoke or retrieve cell phones, so jurors talked among themselves, and took turns pouring cups of the too-strong coffee. Charlie filled a cup from her thermos.

"You got another one of those?" the young lawyer-to-be asked, taking a seat next to her.

"I thought you preferred your caffeine from soft drinks?"

"I do, but today some café au lait sounds soothing. It was getting ugly in the courtroom."

Charlie poured coffee into the small paper cup he held. "It's Clint, isn't it?"

"Yes, but not after Eastwood. My folks were Bill Clinton campaign workers."

"Ah. Your parents, the attorneys. How do you feel you did on the LSAT?"

"I think I did well. Certainly well enough to get into a good law school."

"Where are you thinking of going?"

"There's no thinking to be done. Mom and Dad bleed maize and blue."

"Got it. My father was an attorney. He went to Michigan."

"What about you, Ms. Mack?" The shouted question wafted in from the other side of the room where Richard Fletcher held court with a few other jurors.

"What about me?" Charlie responded, sipping coffee.

"You're a lawyer. You think that lady prosecutor will get a spanking from the judge?"

"I'm not a practicing attorney, Mr. Fletcher, and we're not really supposed to discuss the case."

"I know. I know. But it seems to me, that motel business stirred some things up."

"It probably had more to do with the evidentiary process," Clint piped up.

"You a lawyer, too?"

"No. Not yet."

"Well, what's this evidentiary process business?" Fletcher asked.

Charlie placed her hand on Clint's arm. "I think we need to just wait and see what further instructions we get from the judge."

Fletcher gave Charlie a stony look. The jury foreperson, a fifty-something East Indian man, voiced his agreement with Charlie. An awkward quiet fell over the room, but the fashionista juror broke the frost.

"Well, I'll tell you one thing. I wouldn't mind visiting the Alpine Motel with that fine Allan Bateman."

The laughter came from almost everyone. Clint blushed. The

knitting lady shook her head, and her shoulders bounced with silent chuckling. The tension was broken, and the buzz of conversation picked up again. Fletcher and his two lunch pals moved over to the window seat.

"So, you're going to be a lawyer?" the fashionista woman asked Clint. She filed her nails and gave him a flirty smile.

Clint became unsettled under her stare and leaned back in his chair with a nervous laugh. "That's the plan. Unless I decide to stay in music."

"Music? Are you a singer or something?"

"No, I write music and play guitar."

"Oh."

"My name's Clint by the way." He extended his hand to the young woman and turned on the charm.

"Trina," the girl said, extending her manicured hand. "Lawyers make a lot of money. Musicians don't," she said matter-of-factly.

"That's what my father tells me." Clint shrugged. "He's putting on the pressure."

Trina's judgmental scowl turned into an understanding look. "I know what you mean. My father's a dentist. I work in his office. He thinks I should get a dentistry degree."

"Why don't you?" Clint asked.

"I don't want to spend my days poking in people's mouths," Trina said with a sneer.

And how could you with those nails, Charlie thought, smiling. She watched the give-and-take between the two twenty-somethings for a few minutes. Then she moved to the other side of the table to check on the progress of the afghan.

"That's coming along pretty good. I love the colors."

"Thank you. Yeah, it should take me another week."

"Aw, then I won't get to see the finished product," Charlie said.

"You really think we'll be done by Friday?"

"I sure hope so. I only planned to be away from my office for two weeks."

Charlie watched the jurors at the window seat. They'd been joined by a woman Charlie had heard talk about her son, who had some kind of disability. They spoke in hushed tones and took turns looking over their shoulders.

"It looks like a few people made some friendships during the trial," Charlie noted. "They must have found something they have in common."

"All I ever hear them talk about is money," the knitter said.

"I saw a few of them at the casino during the lunch break. It's kind of hard to resist when we're only a couple of blocks away."

"If you like that sort of thing. My pastor says gambling is a sin."

The judge's clerk stepped into the room. "Okay, they're ready for you again."

"Guess her honor is done with the spanking," Fletcher said in a stage whisper.

A few people snickered as they rose and lined up in the order of their seating. The clerk frowned and scanned them with a warning look. She glanced at her clipboard, satisfied that everyone was in place and then led them to the courtroom.

The judge, both sets of attorneys, and Ms. Raab were already in their places. The ghost was in the courtroom, but Don hadn't returned. Neither had Raab's two gentlemen friends. Spivak took up the questioning while Gleason organized documents at the prosecution table. As Fletcher had speculated, maybe Ms. Gleason had rubbed the bench the wrong way. The judge gaveled the proceedings to order and addressed the jury.

"Ladies and gentlemen, the prosecution failed to follow proper procedure in handling new exhibits. That can happen when there are a lot of documents, and new evidence is discovered and presented. The prosecution and defense attorneys are now all on the same page. We're continuing where we left off, with Ms. Raab's testimony."

"Ms. Raab, have you visited the Alpine Motel?" Spivak asked.

"I have no recollection of that," Raab replied.

Spivak introduced a new exhibit, handing it to Bateman, the judge, and the court reporter.

"Your Honor, may I approach the witness?"

"You may."

Spivak was all business as he stepped toward the witness box. "Ms. Raab, I have a signed declaration from Mr. Kenneth Smith. I'd like you to read it aloud for the jury."

Bateman popped up from his seat. "Your Honor, I see no reason why the witness should be induced to read this document."

"I disagree, Your Honor," Spivak retorted. "Since Ms. Raab is the subject of this exhibit, I think it's highly appropriate."

"Your objection is overruled, Mr. Bateman. Please read the document in front of you, Ms. Raab."

Raab began reciting the incriminating words of Canova's General Manager. The document recounted a series of visits by Ms. Raab and Mr. Smith to the Alpine Motel on Detroit's near east side. The visits were conducted often during the workday, but sometimes in the evening. According to the document, the purpose of the rendezvous often involved the delivery of cash from Mr. Canova to Ms. Raab. However, the visits primarily involved Smith's and Raab's romantic liaisons.

Raab read the document with stony resolve until she got to the last paragraph of the declaration where Smith described Raab's ongoing attempts to rekindle their relationship, even after Canova was indicted on the bribery and conspiracy charges. By the time the witness was done reading, she was in tears.

The courtroom was completely silent. There wasn't even a cough. Charlie swiveled her eyes to watch Goulet. His eyes swept across Canova's back and landed on the sobbing Raab. With a quick glance at the jury, he stood and left the courtroom.

"Do you have any other questions of this witness, Mr. Spivak?" the judge asked.

"Just a couple if the witness can continue."

The judge looked at the courtroom clock and at what Charlie supposed might be a schedule in the folder in front of her. She directed a question to the defense table.

"Will the defense wish to cross-examine this witness?"

"No, Your Honor," Bateman said with resignation.

"Ms. Raab," the judge began, "are you able to continue? If so, you'll be done with your testimony today."

"I . . . I want to finish with this," Raab said. "May I have some water?"

The court clerk quickly found a bottle of water for the witness. Spivak and Gleason conferred for a few more moments, and with a single document in hand Spivak asked for permission to approach the witness. The judge assessed Raab's countenance and beckoned Spivak to continue his examination.

"Ms. Raab, have you ever received money from Kenneth Smith?"

"I refuse to answer on the grounds that it might incriminate me."

Raab resumed invoking her Fifth Amendment rights in response to questions about the Fleetstar executive and Canova's phone records. The prosecution's attempts to connect Raab closer to Canova than she'd earlier testified were thwarted by her declaring her right not to incriminate herself. Within twenty minutes, the judge adjourned for the day, and Ms. Raab's misery, at least in *this* courtroom, was over.

Chapter 9

Charlie was accosted by Judy as she stepped into the office.

"Why didn't you call me? I left you three messages."

"My battery was almost dead, so I turned off my phone after lunch, and didn't think to turn it on when I left the courtroom. It was a grueling day, and I just wanted to get the hell out of there. Where's Don?"

"He's looking for you. I'm calling him now," Judy said, activating the speakerphone.

"Is Gil around?"

"He's here."

"What is it, Novak?" Don answered.

"I've got Charlie here."

"What? How did I miss her?"

"Where are you, Don?"

"A block away from the courthouse. I'm keeping an eye on Goulet's car. He hasn't come out."

"Where'd he go this afternoon?"

"I followed him to the Greektown Casino, and watched him drink. He met a few people at lunch time. Then I followed him to his car, which was parked on Gratiot. He sat in the car for a while; then a black guy arrived and they sat there for another half hour."

"Was it a young guy, short hair, nicely dressed?"

"Yeah."

"I think he's a lawyer."

"He's definitely a lawyer. He works in the Wayne County Prosecutor's Office. I followed the guy back into the courthouse. I know one of the sheriffs, and got an ID from him. The guy's name is Earl Thompson. He's a new attorney there."

"I saw them together earlier today in the courtroom corridor."

"What the hell is going on here, Mack? Why is a prosecuting attorney meeting with a convicted felon in a car?"

"Don, who were the people the ghost met with at the casino?"

"A couple of guys, one white, the other black, and a woman. They sat at a booth at one of the bars, but weren't drinking. They ordered some sandwiches and talked."

"How did they seem? Like they were friends?"

"Hmm. I wouldn't say that. Nobody was laughing. It seemed like they were conducting some kind of business."

"Did they have papers or exchange anything?"

"No. Not that I saw. After they finished eating, the ghost paid the bill and he left the other three there. I followed him back to his car, and that's when he met with the attorney. You got a theory, Mack?"

"Yep. Come on back to the office, Don. Gil's here. I want to talk this over."

"You don't want me to stay with Goulet?"

"Nah. If my theory is right, he'll be back in the courtroom this week."

Charlie made changes to the conference room whiteboard. Caspar Goulet was still in the center in an updated photo Judy had received from the FBI, but the board had a new focus. Charlie had drawn fourteen squares below the photo filled in with either names or descriptors. Charlie was listed in one square, Mr. Fletcher in another. There were squares for the knitting lady, the fashion juror, the man with the beard, Clint, the Blue Cross Blue Shield employee, the jury foreman, and the lady with the disabled son. There were connecting lines drawn to five additional squares. The diagram looked like a two-level organizational chart.

Gil stepped into the conference room and stared at the board. "What's all this?"

"I think Goulet is in the courtroom to bribe the jury on Canova's behalf."

"Hmm. What makes you think that?"

"I'll spell it all out when Don gets here. He's on his way."

Don rushed into the office like a storm trooper. He and Judy immediately started sniping at each other, and as they entered the conference room they were still bickering. Gil and Charlie looked at each other in amusement. Don gawked at the whiteboard for a moment, then lunged for the minibar.

"Don't we have some leftover pizza or something?" he asked, grabbing two bottles of apple juice.

"Hold your horses," Judy said. She opened a lower cabinet, took out a basket with chips, nuts and cheese crackers, and placed it on the table. Don moved for the crackers. Charlie moved to the whiteboard.

"Okay. Here's what I think. The ghost is hanging around the courtroom because he's tampering with the jury. I think he may already have gotten to these three," Charlie said, pointing to squares on the board representing Mr. Fletcher, the lady from Blue Cross and the bearded man. "He may have also gotten to others."

"I'm assuming you still don't want to take your suspicions to law enforcement," Gil said.

"Not yet, Gil. There's really nothing to tell them that I can prove."

"You *could* tell them Goulet is a fugitive, and you know where to find him."

Charlie looked chagrined. "I could, but that wouldn't get to the bottom of things."

"Do you want to get the jurors in trouble?" Judy asked.

"No. Not necessarily. That's not what I'm after."

"What are you after, Mack?"

"I don't know, exactly," Charlie said, taking a seat. "I guess I want to see justice served. That probably sounds kind of idealistic."

"It does actually," Gil said. "But since we all know you, it's not so odd."

"Jury duty helps make our democratic process work. It's the way anybody, regardless of position or class, has a fair path to justice. Now some asshole like Goulet, working for another asshole like Canova, is trying to bypass that process."

"You're right, Mack. You talk like you're running for office. For a minute I thought I heard a fife and drum."

"Very funny, Don. Maybe I *am* making this more about me than it should be. But I need to find out what's going on and I want to snoop for the next couple of days."

"Are you sure, Charlie?" Gil asked.

"I'm sure."

"What do you want me to do?" Judy asked.

"Get me some info on this new prosecutor. What was his name, Don?"

"Earl Thompson."

"Right. Find out where he lives, where he comes from, what law school he went to, how much money he makes, and what his habits are. Let's see if we can figure out why he's hanging around with the ghost."

"Got it," Judy said.

"Don, I want you in court again tomorrow. Come in about ten o'clock. The prosecution should be resting their case, and the defense will take over. If the ghost is working for Canova, he'll come to the courtroom tomorrow. I want you to tail him again. I'd like to know where he goes when he's not in the courtroom. Maybe run his license plate. You got it, didn't you?"

"Yep. I have it."

"What about me?" Gil asked.

"You should stay focused on the Ferry case."

"So that's it. Let's go home. Tomorrow I'll get to know a few more of my fellow jurors."

"Suggestion," Judy said. "Take a couple of bags of candy to share."

"Good idea. Sugar is almost as effective as torture to get people to open up."

"I have another suggestion," Don said. "Don't make any speeches about democracy. Try to act like a normal person."

"Fuck you, Don."

"See. *That's* what I mean. Normal."

Chapter 10

Tuesday

At 7:30 Charlie stepped through the courthouse metal detectors, secured her phone and laptop in a locker, and took the stairs up to the jury room. Taking Judy's advice, she'd brought a package of Hershey's Kisses and a bag of Twizzlers. The kitchen vending area across the hallway was empty, and she opened the cupboard to look for a couple of paper plates. She had to settle for paper cups to hold the Kisses and Twizzlers. Returning to the jury room she found the Blue Cross lady sitting at the table.

"Good morning."

"Good morning," the woman replied and pulled out a book.

"I brought in some candy," Charlie said, filling two cups with the chocolate. She placed one of the cups near the woman. "Help yourself."

"I don't eat much candy," she said.

"Neither do I. Well, that's not true. I never pass up a chance to have a bit of chocolate," Charlie said, smiling. "But this case is making me so restless I needed candy."

The woman returned a slight smile, and looked down at her book.

"My name is Charlene, by the way. I see you're trying to read so I won't bother you anymore."

The woman peeked up at Charlie for a moment. "No problem," she said, closing her book. "I'm Lucille. Lucy."

"Funny, how you can see people every day for a week and not know their names."

"I know. Rich said your name was Charlie."

"Rich?"

"Mr. Fletcher. He said you're a private investigator."

"That's right. It's Charlene, but everyone calls me Charlie."

"Is it interesting work?" Lucy asked, dipping into the cup of Kisses. She took out two pieces and unwrapped the first one.

"Some days it can be very interesting, but mostly it's a lot of sitting around."

"Like what we've been doing the last week?"

"Oh no. This is much worse," Charlie laughed, grabbing a Kiss.

"Jury duty is a pain. They call me every two years like clockwork," Lucy said.

"Didn't I hear you work at the Blues?"

"Uh-huh. My office is right up the street. The good thing is, I have a parking space in the building. So I can just park and walk over."

"Oh, that is lucky. How long have you worked there?"

"Twenty years, and I'm just about burned out."

The bearded white man came in next, stopping abruptly when he saw Charlie and Lucy chatting.

"Good morning," Charlie said. "I brought candy to share."

"Morning," he mumbled, walking quickly past the table to one of the chairs in the back of the room.

Charlie smirked. "I guess he doesn't like candy."

Two more jurors—youngish professional guys—arrived. They had apparently struck up a kinship, because they always sat together in the jury room discussing sports and a video game they both played. One of them was a pure ginger, the other a slight man with salon-cut hair who always wore a pullover sweater atop a collared shirt. Charlie hung her coat over the back of her chair. She hadn't ever said more than hello to the two, but she leaned across the table toward them now.

"I brought in some candy to stave off the boredom."

93

"And you're sharing?" the man with the curly red hair and wisp of a mustache asked.

"Help yourself," Charlie said, pushing the candy in their direction.

"Don't mind if I do," he said, picking up a cup, and shaking a few Kisses into his hand. He offered the cup to his friend, and it was the first time Charlie realized that the two might be gay. His friend shook his head to the offer and pulled a thermos out of his backpack instead.

"You bring in your own coffee?" Charlie asked.

"The stuff in that machine is horrid," the dark-haired guy said dramatically. "This is a special blend I order online."

"Yeah, I've been bringing mine in, too," Charlie said. "But it's probably not as fancy as yours."

"You think the trial will be over by Friday?" the ginger guy asked Charlie while chewing the chocolate.

"God, I hope so. The defense should introduce their witnesses today."

"I hope so too. This twenty-five dollars a day is cramping my style."

"Doesn't your company make up your wages?" Charlie asked nonchalantly.

"Nah. I work for myself. I'm a courier. I'm losing money sitting here."

The jury foreperson and four other jurors, including Clint the law student, the fashion woman, one of the alternates, and the knitting lady entered the jury room within seconds of each other. Almost everyone had accepted the candy, and by ten after eight only a few Twizzlers were left.

"I wonder what this stuff is made of?" Clint asked, putting another one of the gummy, cherry-flavored coils in his mouth.

"You probably don't want to know," the knitting lady said.

Ten minutes later the clerk came into the jury room and did a count. When she didn't like the count, she began a roll call. It was the only one she'd done since the first day of the trial. Richard Franklin was absent, along with the second alternate.

The clerk left the room and Charlie casually reached into her backpack to pull out a paperback. She turned to the last page and jotted all the names she could remember from the roll call.

The knitting lady was Andrews. One of the alternates was called Liss, and the fashion lady was Trina Bradley. Clint's surname was Lakeside, and the curly-haired ginger man answered to Kelly. His gaming pal was Durrell. She hadn't caught the Blue Cross lady's last name, so Lucy would do for now. Add Fletcher and her own name, and she had all but five juror names. She looked around the room determining where to do more snooping. She decided to start with the bearded man who'd been arguing with Fletcher the day before. He was in the corner, in one of the stuffed chairs.

Suddenly, Fletcher rushed into the room like the Kramer character on *Seinfeld*. "I hear I've been holding things up," he said, grinning broadly.

Charlie noted the reaction in the room. A couple of people laughed, but most ignored him. The knitting lady rolled her eyes.

"I brought in candy this morning," Charlie said to Fletcher, gesturing toward the table.

"Ah. Sweets from the sweet."

Mrs. Andrews rolled her eyes again.

In one of their previous conversations, Fletcher had told Charlie he was married. She'd already categorized him as an old-school ladies' man who still thought he had what it took to make a woman's heart flutter. Charlie shot him a fake smile.

The court clerk returned.

"Okay, we're all here now. One of your alternates has called in sick. The judge isn't quite ready for you yet. We're waiting for a witness to arrive. It might be up to an hour wait."

Groans went up around the room. Jurors adjusted themselves for the wait by adding or taking off coats; pulling out crossword puzzles, books and snacks; or moving to one of the wall chairs to have their own company. One of the Kisses cups was being passed around, and the last of the Twizzlers was taken. Charlie grabbed her business card holder from her backpack and approached the bearded man in the corner. He was reading. Charlie caught a glimpse of the cover, a Tom Clancy book.

"Hello. I wanted to give you my card."

The man looked up from his book, annoyed by the interruption. He took the card from Charlie's hand and read it.

"You think I need a private investigator?"

"Not necessarily. But since I'm stuck on jury duty, I'm making the time productive and giving my card to everyone," Charlie lied. "Did you answer to the name Prizzi?"

"Pizzimente. Carl."

"Well, I don't want to interrupt you any further, Mr. Pizzimente. That's a good book. I've read it."

"You like thrillers?"

"I do. I guess it's natural for my line of business. I read thrillers, suspense, crime, and mystery books quite a bit."

"You like Patterson?"

"I've read him. He writes so many I can't keep up."

"I tell you one thing," Pizzimente said with a hint of a smile. "Patterson's legal novels are a *lot* more interesting than this trial."

"I agree with you there."

"But you're a lawyer, I hear, so this must be familiar to you. The waiting and all."

"I don't practice now, but I do know a lot about waiting."

Charlie noticed Fletcher watching them with interest. She excused herself, and returned to her seat at the table. She pulled out her book, turned to the back, and added another name to the list Judy would start checking tomorrow.

Gil arrived in Grand Rapids at ten-thirty in the morning. He located the bar and squared the block once before deciding on a metered space a block away. The Apartment was discreetly decorated, blending in well with the cultural environment of the neighborhood. He knocked at both doors and got no answer. It was a long shot, hoping a bar would be open this early, but he had to be in Kalamazoo this afternoon, and this was his only time to check out this club.

Across the street was a park, and Gil found a bench with a view of the two doors. Sometimes a bar owner or manager would show up early for a liquor delivery, or to start cleaning for the day. Maybe he'd be lucky. Gil was startled when someone he hadn't seen approaching sat down next to him.

"They don't open until two."

His bench companion was a kid, maybe seventeen or eighteen. His blond hair stuck out in a variety of angles, and his blue eyes were the color of ice caps. Although it was cold, he wore sneakers with no socks, and his corduroy coat was only half-buttoned.

"What?"

"The bar. I saw you knocking on the door."

"Where'd you come from?"

The kid nodded over his shoulder toward the other side of the park. "I kinda hang out over there."

"You know the people who run The Apartment?" Gil asked.

"I do odd jobs for them. Mop the floors, stack boxes, help set up the stage area when they need it. Sometimes I help the bartender."

"So you're a regular?"

"You could say that." The boy's eyes flickered a signal to Gil. "You want some action?"

"What?"

"It's early, but I know a place we could use."

Gil understood the boy's meaning and held his stare. Then he stood. "No, I'm not interested in that, but if there's a place around here where we can get a cup of coffee, I'm buying."

Christian was also a regular at the tiny Sheldon Diner, a six-booth hole-in-the-wall catering to the early-morning workers who wanted to order and eat in fifteen minutes or grab breakfast to-go. Gil ordered coffee and a couple of donuts. Christian ordered bacon, eggs, and hash browns. The waiter gave Gil a knowing smile when he brought their food to the booth. Christian said a prayer over his food and then, head still bowed, moved across his plate like a vacuum cleaner. Gil sipped coffee, dunked his donut, and appraised the boy's dirty fingernails and rumpled T-shirt. When the food was consumed, Christian looked up at Gil.

"Sorry. I haven't eaten since yesterday morning."

"No worries. You want my other donut?"

"Can I?"

Gil pushed the plate toward Christian, and pulled a photo of Jason Ferry from his inside jacket pocket.

"You know him?"

The boy lifted the photo, still chomping on a huge piece of donut. He nodded before he could speak.

"That's Jay."

"So, you *do* know him," Gil said, pulling out his notebook.

"Hey. What is this?" Christian said, sitting upright. He looked nervously at the notebook and then squinted. "Hey, are you a cop?"

"I'm not a cop. I'm helping Jason with a problem he's having at school."

The boy's torso relaxed a bit. He gave Gil another once-over, this time with a different motive, and poured more coffee from the carafe.

"I guess I had you wrong."

"No worries. When did you meet Jason?"

"Maybe a year ago. Something like that. He comes to the bar a couple of times a month. When he first started showing up, he kind of kept to himself. Not that many black guys come in, you know?"

Gil nodded.

"But now he fits right in. Is he okay?"

"Yes. But . . ."

"It's his asshole father, isn't it? He's told me about him. We've talked a lot about our dads."

Gil gunned it south on US-131 to Kalamazoo. He was lunching with Jason in the lobby of the hotel where they'd had their first meeting. The highway was dry, the sky was blue, and the engine of Gil's Mustang hummed with the delight of an open road. This far north the tree leaves were a mix of dull October color, but the sun's glint occasionally caught a tree in splendor.

Gil pulled into the hotel parking lot just before one o'clock. He turned off the ignition, but before he could get out of the car, he saw Jason and rolled down the window.

"Man. This is a sweet car," Jason exclaimed.

"You want to sit in it for a minute?"

"Yeah. Can I drive her?"

They eyeballed each other for a couple of beats. Gil stepped out of the car and flipped Jason the keys.

Gil watched as Jason checked the rearview, adjusted the side mirrors, and pushed the seat back a smidgen. "The GT Deluxe V8," he said.

"Yep," Gil answered.

"Sweet."

"Let's go. We can pick up some food and talk in the car."

Gil wasn't surprised that Jason was a skilled and confident driver. When he merged onto I-96, where he could open up the engine, he hit the 80-mph mark before he backed it off to the speed limit. They traded seats when they pulled into a Checkers drive-thru line. They ordered sandwiches, fries and soft drinks, then drove a few miles to a nearby rest stop.

"Let's sit at that picnic table," Gil suggested.

They talked for a few minutes about Gil's discovery of an additional video of Maya's assault. He also told Jason about his conversation with Maya and her friends. It was the same update he'd given Jason's parents.

"How is Maya?"

"She's doing okay. She's a brave girl."

While Jason ate his second burger, Gil counseled the boy on his upcoming grand jury appearance.

"A grand jury is a confidential proceeding. It will look more like a classroom than a courtroom. There are no visitors or other witnesses in the room," Gil said. "Just you, the prosecutor, a court reporter, and twenty-three grand jurors. Your attorneys won't be allowed in the room during your testimony, and the jurors can ask you questions if they want."

"Yeah. Dad's attorney told me," Jason said between bites.

"The prosecuting attorney may or may not bring up the video. But if it comes up, or if they show any of the footage to the grand jurors, that may be your best chance to explain your state of mind during the attack."

"What do you mean?"

"I mean you can tell them what you told me. You didn't like what was going on in that room, and you couldn't wait to get out of there."

"Won't they blame me for not trying to stop it?"

"Maybe. But you're not charged with looking the other way. You're charged with rape, and you didn't commit a rape."

"No. I didn't."

"I spoke to the police again. The detectives investigated all the Gamma members charged in the case."

Jason nodded.

"One of the detectives told me you've been frequently seen at a gay bar. Jason, are you gay?"

The boy leapt from the table, his face contorted in anger, his fists balled. He appeared ready to swing at Gil, who remained seated and expressionless.

"What the fuck did you ask me?" Jason sputtered.

"You heard me, man," Gil replied, keeping his voice low and even.

"That's some bullshit."

"Look, Jason, I don't care if you're gay or not, but it might explain why you're reluctant to say anything about the others. I know you're trying to fit in. I know it can't be easy to be who you are in a fraternity filled with macho jocks."

"I want to go," Jason said, storming off to the car.

Gil picked up their lunch waste and trailed behind the boy. He used the remote to unlock the car and when he slipped behind the wheel, Jason sat sullenly staring out the passenger window.

There was no conversation during the ride back to the hotel parking lot where Jason had left his car. Gil expected the boy to bound from the car as soon as he stopped, but he remained still, and Gil cut the engine.

"I should have helped Maya," Jason said, still staring through the window.

"Yes. You probably should have."

A quiet minute passed. Gil pulled a small cloth from under the seat and began to polish the odometer and radio face.

"My teammates don't know, and my father doesn't know."

"I didn't think so," Gil said, still polishing. "Is there anyone you can talk to about being gay?"

"I have a few friends in Grand Rapids."

"You'll tell people when you're ready. Meanwhile, it's important for you to know that just the way you are is the way you're supposed to be."

Jason didn't say anything for a while, and Gil let him sit in the silence. He shifted the cloth to the cup holder and console.

"I wish Dad would say that to me."

"Your father can be a hard man. I've seen that for myself. But, I also know he has a fierce love for you."

"Do I have to tell the police or the prosecutors I'm gay?" It was the first time since leaving the rest stop that Jason had looked at Gil. "Will they ask me?"

"Even if they know, I don't think they'll ask. It's not relevant to the case. Being gay wouldn't automatically absolve you of raping Maya. You should ask to confer with your lawyer if the prosecutor asks."

Gil let that information sink in with Jason and waited for another question, which didn't come. So, he floated an idea that had occurred to him.

"The more troublesome possibility is that one of the boys in the fraternity, or their lawyers, might try to use the information against you."

"What do you mean?"

101

"If one of the boys who participated in the rape knew your secret, he might ask you to lie for him."

Jason pressed his fists against his eyes. He pounded his head against the headrest. Gil tried to settle the boy with a hand on his shoulder. Jason grasped the door handle, but before he could get it open, he vomited onto his lap and the front seat of the Mustang.

Chapter 11

Tuesday

After a wait of over an hour, the clerk came for the jury. Charlie counted sixteen people in the gallery, among them the ghost and Don. The prosecution called a last-minute surprise witness. Video equipment had been set up at the front of the room, and there was a third lawyer at the government's table. It was the new prosecutor, Earl Thompson, who would question the witness.

"Your Honor, I call Donald Paulsen to the stand."

From the hall, a tall man in a dark suit, burgundy tie, and polished black shoes entered the courtroom and walked up to the witness stand. His bearing and clothing shouted "federal agent." The ghost's shoulders shifted, and he sat upright on full alert. Charlie could almost see a wave of anxiety flow from the crown of his head.

"Mr. Paulsen, what is your occupation?"

"I'm a special agent with the Federal Bureau of Investigation."

"Were you the agent in charge during the surveillance of a meeting last January between Francis Canova and a manager in the city's Department of Purchasing Services?"

"Yes."

Goulet quietly got up from his seat and moved toward the exit. He had to pass a row with two other black-suited men who almost certainly worked for the FBI. Both men looked at the

103

ghost as he passed, but he impeded the view of his face by adjusting his scarf around his neck. Charlie saw Don look back and stand. He had to wait for a lady to move her bag before he could exit his row, and his face flushed with impatience. As he moved to the door, Don also received the FBI once-over.

"Mr. Paulsen, I'd like you to walk the jury through the video you and your agents captured on the evening of Tuesday, January 18, 2005."

"Okay."

The monitor showed a nighttime meeting, shot through a restaurant window, of a man easily identified as Canova and an overweight man in a Columbo-like beige raincoat. The video had no sound. The man nervously downed a glass of what looked like wine. Canova sipped at his wine, and ten minutes into the tape a waiter brought a plate of food, which Canova ate with relish.

"This is at nineteen-hundred hours on the eighteenth." The agent caught himself. "That's 7 p.m.," he said in the direction of the jury. "Canova is the man on the left; Robert Widdon is the man on the right. Widdon is the executive charged with the oversight of Detroit's vendor licenses. He reports to Adrienne Raab. We were tipped off to this meeting by an anonymous call, and we obtained a court order to surveil Mr. Widdon and wire the restaurant."

With no warning, the audio on the tape sounded loudly, and the agent fumbled with the remote to decrease the volume. The jury continued watching the restaurant scene, and the sound was surprisingly clear.

You should have ordered some food. I know the rules about gifts from vendors. But there's no rule about eating, is there?

Canova had a cackling laugh, which Charlie found repulsive. He took a huge gulp of wine, and wiped his napkin roughly across his mouth.

I'm not hungry. I just want to take care of the matter we discussed and get out of here.

Canova stared at Widdon, and the man seemed to shrink under his gaze.

Okay, okay. People don't know how to conduct business anymore.

Charlie leaned forward to see when Canova pulled what looked like a menu from the condiments rack and handed it to Widdon. The man began to protest until Canova pointed to the menu.

Open it!

Widdon's eyes grew wide as he emptied the contents of the menu, and shoved his hand inside his rumpled coat. Just as suddenly as it began the sound dropped out again.

"Okay, we lost audio again at this point," the special agent explained unnecessarily. "But Mr. Widdon can be seen here removing an envelope from the menu, and he puts it into his jacket pocket."

Widdon hurriedly stood and looked around the restaurant before bolting for the door. Canova pushed his plate away and drained the wine in his glass. He refilled his glass from the bottle on the table and took a cell phone from his pocket.

"Okay. Our audio is still defective at the beginning of this phone call, but the sound returns in a moment," the agent said.

. . . don't know. He's a pussy.

He wouldn't even eat, and he downed that expensive wine like he was tasting gasoline.

Don't send me these peons anymore. Next time I only want to deal with the head lady.

Yeah. Five grand. Yeah, I'm gonna finish my wine and then go on home. I'll see you in the morning.

"That's the end of our surveillance tape," the agent said, punching a button on the remote to close the video.

"Agent Paulsen, what is in the envelope that Mr. Widdon received?" Thompson asked

"We believe it to be cash."

"Who is Mr. Canova speaking to on the phone in the video?"

"We've identified the person as Harvey Rush, Mr. Canova's accountant."

"Thank you, Agent Paulsen. I have no further questions," the young prosecutor said.

105

"Cross-examination, Mr. Bateman?" the judge asked.

"Yes. I have a few questions." Bateman stood at the defense table. "Agent Paulsen, did you follow Mr. Widdon after he left the restaurant?"

"I'm not at liberty to say. That information is part of an on-going investigation."

"You insinuated that Mr. Canova passed an envelope of cash to Mr. Widdon. Do you have proof that money exchanged hands?"

"It's obvious, isn't it?"

"Not to me," Bateman said dramatically.

The agent smirked and leaned back in his seat.

"Agent Paulsen, do you know the name of the person Mr. Canova alluded to in the phone call as 'the head lady'?"

"We have reasons to believe it is Ms. Raab in the city's Department of General Services."

"What reasons are those?"

"We have additional surveillance evidence."

"Are we going to see any of that evidence?"

"No. Because it's part of another ongoing investigation."

"But that evidence won't be presented in court today. Is that correct?"

"Correct."

"So it can't be considered in this case," Bateman said, looking directly at the jury. "No further questions of this witness, Your Honor."

The judge stared at Thompson. Spivak and Gleason also stared at their new colleague, but he remained motionless, staring down at his legal pad.

"Do you wish to redirect, Mr. Thompson?" the judge asked impatiently.

Thompson signaled "no" with a head shake, and began to stand, but Spivak leaped from his chair. "Your Honor, may we approach the bench?"

"Approach," the judge said.

Charlie watched the defense and prosecuting attorneys gather in front of the bench. The judge activated the white noise in the courtroom, cloaking the conversation, and leaned toward the group. They conferred for only a few minutes, with Spivak doing most of the talking. The judge directed a comment toward Thompson, whose shoulders slumped. Then Harrington-Smoot said something to Bateman, who nodded his agreement. The judge silenced the white noise and the attorneys returned to their respective tables. Bateman whispered something to Canova. At the prosecutor's table, Spivak remained standing while Gleason and Thompson sat.

"We have another question, Your Honor."

"Proceed, Mr. Spivak."

"Mr. Paulsen, isn't it a matter of record that a grand jury has voted to indict Mr. Widdon on charges of bribery and conspiracy?"

"And collusion. Yes."

"Thank you, Mr. Paulsen. *Now* we have no further questions," Spivak stated with a glower for his colleague. "The prosecution rests, Your Honor."

The judge looked over her glasses at the defense table. "Mr. Bateman, are you ready to begin?"

Bateman stood. "Your Honor, may we have a half-hour recess before we begin?"

"I don't see any reason why not," Judge Harrington-Smoot said. "We'll take our morning break now. Twenty minutes."

A substantial break meant the smokers could head downstairs to the patio and others to their communications devices, so the jury room was sparsely occupied. Charlie watched Mrs. Andrews work away on her afghan, her needles clicking in the quiet of the room. Clint was showing the fashion girl, Trina Bradley, pictures of his gig last year in Brazil. The foreperson sat at the head of the table reading. Charlie had learned his name was Mr. Naidu by peeking at the jury sign-in sheet he signed each morning. The alternate juror sat slumped in one of the comfy chairs. He always seemed to be sleeping when they weren't in the courtroom, and Charlie had seen him yawn a couple of times during the video viewing.

Charlie walked over to the window seat with her thermos and poured a cup. She peered down into the courtyard where Fletcher, Lucy the insurance lady, Mr. P. the reader of thrillers, and the redheaded courier were in conversation. None of them appeared to be smoking. Charlie moved back to the conference table. She looked at the sleeping alternate, but decided he wouldn't appreciate being awakened to receive a business card. So she sat down next to Mr. Naidu.

"Hi. I'd like to give you one of my cards. Since this is our last week together, I thought I'd better let people know about my services."

Naidu smiled, looked at the card, and smiled again. He put the card in his breast pocket. "Thank you, Ms. Mack."

"Do you enjoy being the foreman?"

"I am used to having responsibilities."

"So you must be the boss of a company?"

"No. Nothing like that. I am a counselor to my family, and I'm on the board of the community center in my neighborhood."

"I see. I can tell you take your jury job very seriously."

"Yes. But not everyone does. This is not a place for jokes and frivolity."

"I think people are just bored."

"A man's life and livelihood are at stake. That is very serious."

"People just stopped doing the right thing," Mrs. Andrews announced, obviously overhearing their conversation. She sat at one of the side chairs behind the conference table. "I taught school for thirty years, and I tell you people have changed."

Charlie sat in the chair next to Andrews to admire her work. "That's a beautiful pattern. You really know what you're doing."

"I've had a lot of time to practice since I retired."

Charlie scanned the table. The other jurors seemed preoccupied, either with conversation or some other activity. She leaned in closer to Mrs. Andrews.

"I have a question for you. It may seem odd."

"That's okay."

"Has anyone from the outside approached you wanting to talk about this case?"

Andrews looked up quickly from her knitting and then returned to it with only two seconds of break in her rhythm. "Yep."

Charlie lowered her voice. "Did anybody offer you money to vote a certain way?"

Andrews didn't break from her handiwork this time. She joined Charlie in whispering. "I told that guy he was a crook, and he didn't have enough money in this world to buy my integrity. He pretended he was only making a joke, but I know he meant it."

Charlie wanted to ask another question, but she noticed the fashionable Trina squinting her heavily mascaraed eyes their way.

"Like I said before," Andrews said. "People have changed."

Chapter 12

Tuesday

The Mustang was parked in a stall at the self-serve car wash. Gil always carried rags, a small bottle of pine cleaner, a scrub brush, tire polish, and a small pail in his trunk—for emergencies. Jason had already done a good job of flushing the floor mats and cleaning the seat. Now he was following Gil's directions on how much disinfectant to put in the pail for the final wipe down.

"Might as well clean the outside since we're here," Gil said.

They circled the vehicle like doctors in an operating suite—washing, drying, polishing, pointing to missed spots, and finally sharing a satisfied smile at their handiwork.

"She's looking good," Jason said.

"Okay, now let's do yours," Gil offered.

Jason's silver 2006 Acura had been a high school graduation gift from his parents. The car didn't need much attention on the outside. They soaped and rinsed it, then moved it next to Gil's Mustang in the adjacent lot to dry it and do some inside detailing.

"I'm sure you have other things to do," Jason said as he wiped his mats and dashboard with Gil's pine cleaner.

Gil squatted to spray foam on the front tire. "Washing the car helps to clear my mind. I've had some great epiphanies that way."

"My mother always said she wished I'd spent as much time cleaning my room as I did the family cars." Jason laughed.

"You and your mother seem to have a pretty good relationship."

"Yep. She's cool."

"Does she know you're gay?" Gil didn't look up from the tire. He let the void that followed his question reach its natural conclusion.

"Once when I was a kid, we talked about me liking one of the boys in my school. She's never asked me about it since, but I think she knows."

Gil moved to squat at the back tire. "Hey, throw me the scrub brush, will you?"

Jason came to the rear of the car holding the brush and pail.

"What do you think?" Gil asked, gesturing with both hands to present the tire.

"Looks good, man."

"The secret to a nice-looking tire is to put a splash of furniture polish in the water. It's a trick I learned from my uncle. He sells cars."

"Cool." Jason shoved his hands into his pockets. So, are *you* gay?"

"Nope."

"But you think it's okay that *I* am?"

Gil pondered what he should say: *It's not my business. Who am I to judge? I have friends who are gay.* He finally decided on: "We love who we love."

"I don't think the feelings I have are about love. You know?"

"They will be one day."

The rest of the morning and afternoon in the courtroom progressed with benign boredom. Between the dull testimony and Ms. Andrews' revelation, Charlie had a hard time concentrating.

Bateman introduced a series of witnesses from Canova's operation to refute the evidence provided by the defendant's former accountant and chauffeur. Spivak was back in action as the lead prosecutor, and in cross-examination he punched away at the defense witnesses, but didn't land any blows.

Goulet and Don hadn't returned to the courtroom, and at lunchtime Charlie walked to a nearby Starbucks to call the office. Judy hadn't heard from Don, but she'd made good progress on digging up information about the newbie prosecutor, Earl Thompson.

"He just moved to Detroit last year. He worked for a firm in Baltimore for five years after graduating from law school in DC."

"Did you find out anything about his friends, his habits, that sort of thing?"

"I've been scanning the newspapers and press services, and I picked up a few things but I'll keep looking. I've ordered a credit report and criminal report through our usual provider, and I'm waiting on that."

"Great, keep it up."

"Also, I heard from Gil. He's in Kalamazoo and will call when he's on his way back."

"Fine. Meanwhile, the candy worked like a charm. I have more juror names for you to check out."

Chapter 13

Tuesday

For the remainder of the afternoon, Allan Bateman's defense strategy was to show that his client was a philanthropist using his cash-driven business to support many worthwhile causes. Much of that altruism, argued Bateman, involved giving away gobs of cash in a manner that might have the appearance of pay-offs. Three witnesses swore that they were the recipients of Canova's generosity.

The trial was adjourned for the day at four, and the ghost had not showed up again. Charlie retrieved her belongings and walked away from the main door of the courthouse before she stopped in the doorway of a building to check her phone messages. Mandy had called suggesting they eat out for dinner. Judy's message, ten minutes ago, was to let her know Gil was in the office and had things to report. There was no message from Don.

Charlie pulled up the collar of her coat and started walking again. She stopped short when she recognized Don's unoccupied car at a parking meter across the street. She tried his cell phone, and when he didn't answer, walked over to the Buick. It was locked and undisturbed. She started walking again, and had gone a half-block when she sensed someone behind her. She spun, ready to defend herself.

"Whoa, Mack. It's just me."

"Don, where the hell did you come from?"

"You should see your face. You look ready to take me out."

"You know better than to sneak up on me," Charlie shot back, not smiling.

"Sorry. I understand why you're mad."

Charlie trembled, trying to shake off the memory of waking up bound and gagged, lying in an overgrown lot after being knocked unconscious and left for dead. It was a recurring memory, thankfully coming up less often these days.

"I saw your car. Where were you?"

"I was in a bush in the back of the Murphy building."

"What?"

"I've been following Goulet. When he left the courtroom, he drove to a house where I think he lives. He was there for hours, and I was bored as shit. Then at three-thirty, he comes running out of the house, and I followed him back here. I had to look for him for a minute, but I finally saw him through a door that leads out onto some kind of courtyard. He looked like he was waiting for someone, and I didn't want to get caught hanging around, so I found a spot on the side of the building where I could see into the yard."

"I'm surprised you weren't nabbed by security."

"Yeah, well, security ain't what it used to be. Especially at closing time."

"Did he meet with Thompson? Judy's dug up a few things about him."

"No. I didn't see him. I *did* see the guy he met with at the casino."

"Which one?"

"The black guy. What's his name?"

"Fletcher."

"Right. Him. There was also a good-looking younger girl, not the one I saw at the casino, and another guy—red hair with beady eyes."

"That would be Kelly, the courier.

"How would you describe the girl?"

"Like I said, pretty. A lot of hair and fancy high heels."

"Trina, the fashionista. What were they doing, Don?"

"Smoking and talking. Fletcher was doing most of the talking, but the girl was making her points, too."

Charlie closed her eyes a second to catch the thought that sped across her brain. "I wonder how the ghost knew when to come back to the courtroom?"

"Educated guess? Don't you usually end the day at four?"

"Most of the time. But not always. Let's head to the office to debrief."

Gil described, in detail, his achingly emotional meeting with Jason. There wasn't much to say in response, but Don had a reaction.

"At least he helped you clean up the Mustang."

Charlie, Judy and Gil glared at Don. Charlie had given up being surprised by some of the insensitive things that came out of Don's mouth, but he still managed to stun her from time to time.

"That's the only thing you have to say about this boy's pain?" Judy said, unable to help herself, then turning her shoulder to Don as she'd done so many times before. "Do you plan to tell Jason's father about your conversation?" Judy asked Gil.

Gil shook his head. "It's not my place. Jason has to be the one to tell his father about his sexual orientation. But a few people are aware now that Jason's gay, so he better not wait long."

"That'll be a tough conversation," Charlie said. "Maybe he could talk to his mother first."

"I made the same suggestion to him," Gil said.

Charlie shifted the meeting to the Canova trial. "There was an FBI witness on the stand today. Goulet looked like he was going to have a heart attack when he realized feds were in the court-room."

Don nodded in agreement. "He slunk out of there like a turkey two days before Thanksgiving."

"I'm surprised he takes the chance of being in a courthouse where there's bound to be all kinds of law enforcement," Gil said.

"He's probably using an alias." Don pulled himself closer to the table and turned pages in his notebook. "Plus, he really doesn't look much like that photo the FBI gave us. He's thinner now, wears glasses, and has shaved his head. I followed him to a house at 11415 Periwinkle Street in Taylor. Might be where he lives. He was there for several hours, and nobody else came or left. Then, like I told Charlie, he came running out at three-thirty, and I followed him back to Murphy courthouse. He parked, went in, and I watched from behind a hedge as he talked to some of Charlie's jurors in the smoker's courtyard."

"How do we find out what name he's using now?" Charlie asked. "Anybody who comes into the visitors' door at the court-house has to show ID. You think they scan those?"

Charlie's question was met with "are you kidding?" stares.

"Why don't we start with the records for the house on Peri-winkle," Judy offered, "and Don running the plates on his car."

"Right, I still need to make that call," Don said, taking a note.

"So, here's something," Charlie said. "One of the jurors today confirmed my suspicion about bribery. She said she was waiting at the bus stop, and a man started talking to her about her jury vote."

"Was it Goulet?" Gil asked.

"She said she'd hadn't seen him at the courthouse, before or after he spoke to her, but she suspects some of the others have also been approached."

"Did she say who?"

"The same ones Don saw chatting with the ghost today."

"I guess that proves you're right-on about the jury tampering," Gil said.

"I think we should investigate the rest of the jurors," Charlie suggested.

"Why? Isn't that getting into tricky legal waters?"

"I don't think so. There's a presumption that jurors are anony-mous, but the first amendment allows the public to know jurors' names. Think about it; anybody sitting in the courtroom can identify jurors, at least by sight."

"But if you're right that the ghost, or somebody working for him, is contacting certain jurors and not others, he has a lot more information than just what you all look like," Don noted.

"Right. So where's he *getting* his information? Is he doing his own research like us?"

Charlie moved to the whiteboard, and pulled out a red marker. She wrote and circled a name.

"Earl Thompson," Judy read aloud.

"Maybe it's the junior prosecutor feeding info to Goulet."

"That's a reasonable theory," Gil agreed.

Judy opened a folder, and distributed copies of the one-sheeter she'd created. "Here's what I know about Thompson so far."

"This is a great summary," Charlie said, reading. "How'd you discover he's the youngest in a family of eight?"

"I found an article in his hometown paper in Arkansas. It was a small-town-boy-makes-good sort of thing."

"I never even heard of this city where he was born," Don said.

"You'd probably have to be Bill Clinton to have heard of it," Judy quipped.

"He certainly lives at a fancy address," Gil noted. "That's one of the new buildings on the Detroit riverfront."

"And he's a man-about-town," Judy added. "I found a half-dozen news clippings about his social activities. That's not in the summary, but I have the copies."

"Let me see those," Don said, reaching. "Yep, he's the one I saw in Goulet's car."

"His credit score isn't too impressive," Gil said. "Not for a single guy with the salary he makes. He's probably overextended. That would make him vulnerable to someone who wants to pay for information."

"Okay. I want to find out fast which jurors have probably taken bribes," Charlie said.

"Will they have to go to jail?" Judy asked.

"I don't know. What's the law on that, Gil?"

Gil laced his fingers across his chest. "Well, jury tampering is a felony. But there's also a charge called Bribe Received by a

Juror, or something like that. I think it's still a felony, but maybe a different class. I'll have to look it up."

"Judy, here are the other juror names I was able to dig up. I'm not sure the spellings are correct. Tomorrow, see what you can find out about them. Concentrate first on Mr. Fletcher, the lady who works for Blue Cross—her last name's Murphy—and this Pizzimente guy."

"You want me to stay with the ghost?" Don asked.

"Yes. I need proof of a direct link between him and Frank Canova."

"And I guess I'm staying with the Ferry case," Gil said.

"Right. It's the work that's actually bringing in money."

Charlie sat next to Mandy in a back booth at their favorite Mexican restaurant. They both had giant salt-rimmed margaritas, and they shared chips and salsa while waiting for their food. The tables at the neighborhood haunt were filled with jovial diners. Animal-shaped piñatas and strings of peppers hung from the ceiling, and the entire room glowed from the year-round Christmas lights strung along the windows and the chair rail. What the eatery lacked in imaginative décor was offset by the authentic, fresh, and tasty entrees created and dished up by the owner's wife in the *cocina*.

"Another margarita?" the waiter asked as he placed sizzling fajita combination platters on the table. The steam from the grilled steak and chicken pushed Charlie and Mandy back against the bench.

"Not for me. I'm driving," Charlie said.

"Well, I'm not. So, 'si' to another margarita." Mandy smiled.

They dug into their food—elbows bumping—for two minutes before Charlie picked up the conversation where they'd left off.

"So, I think the ghost has bribed some of the jurors."

"Have you seen any money pass hands?" Mandy asked, capturing rock salt on her tongue.

"Stop doing that."

"What?"

"Sticking your tongue out like that. It makes me so hot."

"It's probably just the salsa verde making you hot. Come on, answer my question."

"I haven't seen any exchange of money. But there's a group who regularly gathers to whisper. Don saw several of them talking to this Goulet guy—first at the casino bar, then today in the courthouse patio. I'm putting two and two together."

"But you can't prove it."

"Mrs. Andrews says she was offered a bribe."

"But she also told you it wasn't Goulet who approached her. It was someone else."

"Right. I think the only way to get proof is to show my hand."

"What do you mean?"

"I think I just have to straight up accuse one of them of taking a bribe."

"You think someone will admit to it?"

Charlie took a break from eating to think. She watched Mandy hold a flour tortilla across the palm of her hand, and systematically scoop a mix of steak and chicken, pico de gallo, guacamole, and sour cream into the center of the tortilla. She rolled the tortilla into what looked like a blunt, tucked the ends, then carefully cut it in half, pushing back the overflowing contents with her knife. Taking a big bite of her makeshift burrito, she chased it with a forkful of beans and chewed contentedly, rewarding her efforts with a long sip of her drink.

"Have I ever told you that watching you eat is like having an orchestra seat at a Broadway musical?"

"You're not going to break into a *Sweeney Todd* song, are you?"

"I would if Judy were here." Charlie smiled at her girlfriend, then changed topics. "Look, I know the whole thing sounds weird."

"What whole thing?"

"Trying to figure out this jury tampering business."

"No, it doesn't sound weird. It sounds obsessive. You have Don following this guy around, and you're checking into people's backgrounds like some client is paying you, and they're not. Ultimately, you have to tell the judge or somebody and it will all lead to a mistrial. Why not just do that now?"

"I could be wrong. You said it yourself. I don't have proof."

"You're probably not wrong. The knitting lady confirmed your suspicions, and that guy in the courtroom is a red flag."

Charlie sliced up some steak and chicken, mixed it with a pile of rice and shoved it into her beans. She tore off a piece of tortilla, and with the aid of a fork scooped the mix onto the tortilla and into her mouth.

"Olé." Mandy roared at Charlie's technique. Then she got quiet. She put her fork down until Charlie looked her in the eye. "Why are you pursuing this? What do you hope to accomplish?"

"To see justice served."

"If you talk to the judge tomorrow, you'll have done all that's expected of you."

"What's expected has never been enough for me. You should know that by now."

"You want to put the Corvette in the garage?" Mandy asked as they pulled up to the house.

"Nah. I'll leave it in the driveway. I'll be heading out before you in the morning."

"Okay. I'm going to walk Hamm. You want to come?"

"If you don't mind, no. Judy phoned. I want to call her back before it gets too late." Charlie leaned over to kiss Mandy. "You're right, Hon. I *have* become obsessed with this courtroom drama. I'll ask to speak to the judge tomorrow."

Stepping through their front door, they were greeted by Hamm with jumps and twirls and frantic tail wags. He was a pleasant mix of Labrador and some other more high-strung breed. His welcome was always enthusiastic, but tonight it was driven by his need for the outdoors.

"Okay, my boy, we're going for a walk," Mandy said, using her baby-talk voice and grabbing the leash.

Charlie rubbed Hamm's head and pushed his excited bottom to the floor so Mandy could connect the leash to his collar.

"We'll be right back. Tell Mommy we'll be right back," Mandy cooed, closing the front door.

Charlie sat at the kitchen counter to call Judy, who answered on the first ring.

"I got the information you wanted on most of the names."

"Wait, Judy. I've decided we're not going to do any more investigating on the trial. Tomorrow morning I'll send the judge a message about improprieties with the jury, and we'll be out of it. Sorry to put you to so much trouble."

"No worries. All part of a day's work. Have you discussed it with Don?"

"Not yet."

"He's out tracking the ghost right now, isn't he?"

"That won't be a waste of time. We'll be able to give the FBI specific information about Goulet's whereabouts and his activities of the last couple of days. That's a favor that might come in handy later. But I better call Don now."

"Okay, Charlie. See you tomorrow?"

"Probably early. I doubt I'll be on jury duty after I speak with the judge."

Charlie took a deep breath before dialing Don's number. He wouldn't be so understanding about standing down. He was hours into evening surveillance work, and he hated sitting around in a car.

"What is it, Mack?" Don answered grumpily.

"How are you doing?"

"I'm bored and hungry. I'm parked up the street from a restaurant in Bloomfield Hills where ten minutes ago Allan Bateman was having a drink with Frank Canova and the ghost. They were all thick as thieves."

"Or put another way, it's a billable attorney-client meeting."

"I'm sticking with thieves. Because after celebrity lawyer Bateman left, guess who showed up?"

"One of the jurors?"

121

"No."

"Are you gonna make me guess?"

"Assistant prosecutor Earl Thompson. He's in there now."

"Damn! Can you get a photo?"

"I don't think so. There's no way to walk in without being seen. It's kind of a fancy place . . ."

Charlie jumped from her seat as the front door crashed open, shaking the walls. Mandy was screaming. Charlie dropped the phone and ran to the front of the house where she was met by a blast of cold air and a wide-eyed shaken Mandy.

"Charlie," she sobbed. Her coat was ripped. Her face had wide red blotches and was smudged with dirt. "They took Hamm."

Chapter 14

Tuesday

Charlie gripped the wheel of the Corvette with white knuckles. Despite the piercing cold from the open window, she wiped sweat from her eyes. They'd been circling the area for an hour looking for Mandy's attacker. Every joint, every muscle, in Charlie's body was tensed with fury, and the gun nestled in her lap gave her resolve. She looked away from the street at Mandy, who sat stony-faced and somber, curled in on herself and pressed against the passenger door.

"I should have been able to stop him." Mandy's voice was raspy.

"It happened too fast."

"If only I'd had my gun."

Mandy had been frantic when she'd burst through the front door, quickly pulled herself from Charlie's embrace, and grabbed at the car keys. Charlie had only seconds to retrieve her gun from the hall closet and convince Mandy she was still too shaken to drive. They sped the three blocks to the spot where a man driving a late-model Mercedes had pulled to the curb, rolled down the window, and called Mandy by name.

She'd pulled at the leash to slow Hamm, pausing to peer at the man in the shadows of the front seat, and had no time to react when the back seat passenger threw open the door and charged at her. Mandy backpedaled, falling against a tree. Hamm sprung forward in protective mode, but was stopped short by the leash looped around Mandy's wrist. Hamm's lunges wouldn't allow Mandy to regain her footing, and she cried out as she slammed into the tree several times. Hamm's furious barking and Mandy's shouts drew the attention of people in nearby houses, and front porches suddenly lit up. The assailant kicked Hamm, and he yelped in pain and fell to the ground. Then the man hit Hamm in the head with a rock loosened from the tree box ledge. Mandy pushed to her knees to spring at the man, and that's when he aimed a gun at her head.

"Stop," he yelled, unclipping the leash from Hamm's collar. "Tell your partner to back off and mind her own business. This is a warning." Without another word he dragged Hamm, stunned and hurting, into the Mercedes and it careened down the street.

Charlie's phone rang, and she put it on speaker.

"Don?"

"Mack, I'm in front of your house. Where are you?"

"Mandy and I are looking for the son of a bitch."

"Did she get the plate?"

"No. Everything happened so fast."

"Mack, both of those goons are long gone. They'd never stay in your neighborhood."

"We thought they might put Hamm out of the car. He was hurt." Charlie teared up.

"Come back to the house and we'll figure out what to do."

Grosse Pointe Park Detective Gino Solis sat across the kitchen counter from Charlie, Mandy, and Don. He wrote notes as Mandy recounted the details of the assault. Charlie had dabbed an antibacterial ointment on the scrapes on Mandy's hands and cheek, but her torn shirt was streaked with grime and the back of her red hair was matted with tree bark and grass.

"We're going to record it as an assault and battery," Solis said. "Strictly speaking this is Detroit jurisdiction, but because you're one of ours, we'll claim the case and put it on the front burner. I'll have a couple of uniforms go back to the scene in the morning, check the tree box for any evidence, and talk to the neighbors on that block. This isn't much of a description: Black, six feet tall, skinny build, dark clothes."

"Sorry. I was getting bounced around, and by the time I could focus on the guy, he was holding a gun, which got all my attention."

"You didn't get a look at the driver at all?"

Mandy shook her head. "It was too dark."

"Perhaps one of the neighbors got a better look or saw the license plate. I'm sure people were at their windows if porch lights came on."

"Maybe," Mandy said somberly.

"Tell me again what this man said to you. 'Tell your partner this is a warning?' Was he referring to Charlie?"

"I think so."

"What's *that* all about?" Solis shifted his question to Charlie. "Are you on some case that's put you in trouble?"

"We're not sure," Charlie lied.

"Do you want a patrol car outside?"

"That won't be necessary, Solis," Don spoke up quickly. Then, understanding from the looks he got that it really wasn't his call, he held up his hands apologetically.

"I don't think there'll be any more problems tonight," Mandy said.

Solis looked like he might protest, but thought better of it. He closed the notebook, and scanned the grim faces across from him.

"Well, I guess that's that. You got a shift tomorrow?"

"Uh huh. But I think I'm calling out," Mandy said.

"Understandable."

"Gino, would you also alert the patrols to look out for our dog? Here's his picture."

The detective looked at the photo and tucked it into his notebook. "Sure thing. I'll make sure DPD has the photo too. Who knows, if they release Hamm he may find his way back home. Dogs can do that, you know."

125

Mandy walked Solis to the door. It was almost midnight. Judy was standing by at home for a conference call, and Gil had insisted on coming to the house. When Mandy returned to the kitchen, she'd added a heavy cardigan sweater over her shirt, which she pulled tightly across her body.

"I'm cold."

Charlie reached for Mandy's hand. "Why don't you take a shower or a hot bath? I'm going to have a quick meeting with the team. Gil's on his way over."

"What are you up to, Charlie?"

"Three hours ago, my intent was to report to the courthouse tomorrow and tell the judge everything I know."

"And now?"

"Now, I intend to make the people who attacked you, and took Hamm, very sorry for what they've done."

"Let's not make things any worse than they already are," Mandy said, gripping the sweater tighter.

"They pointed a gun at you," Charlie said, slamming her hand on the table.

"And if I'd had my revolver," Mandy said, "I probably would have shot one, or both, of those guys and I'd be on administrative leave. Let's not escalate things. If you plot some revenge against these men and carry it out, you'll have your own trouble."

Mandy spoke loudly, her eyes squinted in anger. "We should have given Solis the whole story. He's no fool. He could tell something else was going on."

Don excused himself to go the restroom. Charlie pulled out a stool for Mandy, but she shook her head and remained standing.

"Do you want some tea?"

"No. But I'm going to take that hot bath you suggested."

"Mandy, I'm really sorry. We'll get Hamm back." Charlie reached out for Mandy, who took a step back.

"Don't you see, Charlie? All of this connects back to your ego. It wasn't enough for you to inform the judge about irregularities with the jury. You had to start snooping and be the one to catch the bad guys. I blame you that Hamm is gone."

"I don't want Mandy involved. It could jeopardize her job." Charlie looked at Don and Gil, sitting at the kitchen counter, who nodded agreement.

"Charlie, read the text message you received again?" Judy asked through the speakerphone.

Don't make trouble for us on the trial. Just stay out of our way, and we'll let your dog go.

"Who are these fuckers?" Gil asked.

"Canova's henchmen, or Goulet's. Somebody who's doing their dirty work," Don said.

"I think someone in the jury room overheard my conversation with Mrs. Andrews and tipped off the ghost."

"That Fletcher guy," Don guessed.

"Or the fashion girl. She seemed to be watching us."

"You think these jurors would condone violence?" Judy asked.

"They probably haven't considered anything beyond the promise of a payoff," Charlie said. "But Thompson must be aware of the kind of men he's dealing with. As a prosecutor, his crime is *worse* than the jurors'."

"What about Bateman?" Judy asked. "You think he knows about the jury tampering?"

"I'd like to think he wouldn't go along with something like this. Whatever happens to Canova, he's still got his reputation as a defense attorney to protect," Gil answered.

"That's all well and good, but Bateman had dinner tonight with Canova and Goulet. I saw him. If you don't want fleas, don't sleep with dogs," Don quipped.

Charlie rubbed her palms against her eye sockets. She was still electric with anger and could feel the pulsing of her blood behind her eyes. She took a few deep breaths, and leaned into the back of her stool, letting her arms dangle at her side.

"Mandy blames me for what happened to Hamm."

"She doesn't really mean that, Mack; she's just upset," Don said.

Charlie shook her head. "She's right in a way. If I'd gone to the judge with my suspicions, we wouldn't be in this spot."

"Don's right," Judy said through the speaker. "Mandy's hurt, embarrassed, and worried about Hamm. She'll get over it."

Gil was watching Charlie. "What are you thinking?"

"I'm not going to jury duty tomorrow. Instead, I want to pay a surprise visit to the ghost, and I'm going to beat him until he tells me where Hamm is."

"Then what?" Don asked.

"Then we take him to the FBI. After that, I'll go to the court-house, talk to the judge, and tell her about the rotten jurors assigned to her trial."

"Frank Canova may be a small-time gangster, but he's still dangerous," Gil said. "Think about it. He probably has Goulet on his payroll, and the two guys from tonight. He knew about Mandy, has your cell phone number, probably has your address, and who knows what else."

"And I have *his* address," Don said. "I followed Canova home from the restaurant."

"Good, Don," Charlie said.

"I'm with Gil." Judy's voice sprung from the speakerphone. "You don't want to put your home and family in any more danger."

"It's too late. Mandy was in danger. As far as I'm concerned, this is war." Charlie spit out the words.

"Then let's treat it like war," Gil said. "That means we pick our battles and our targets. We have to be strategic. I know you're angry, but what's the most important thing to do right now?"

"Kick Goulet's ass," Don answered.

"No," Charlie said, shaking her head. "It's not. The important thing is to get Hamm back."

"Won't we have to rough up the ghost to get him back?" Don asked.

"That'll be up to him," Charlie responded.

Chapter 15

Wednesday

Now that the stakes on the jury trial had been raised to a personal level, Charlie had to pull rank to keep Gil focused on the Ferry case. He wasn't happy about it, but finally conceded that with Jason's grand jury appearance scheduled for Monday, it was impractical for him to be involved in the rescue of Hamm.

That morning, he'd been summoned to the Ferry house for an emergency meeting, and was en route to Palmer Park. He couldn't reach Judy to report his change in schedule, so he tried Charlie's mobile phone. When she didn't answer, he called her home number. He was about to hang up when Mandy finally answered.

"Hello?"

"Mandy, it's Gil. How are you doing?"

"Don't ask."

"No word from the police?"

"No. And Charlie won't return my calls."

"I tried to reach her, too."

"I'm furious." Mandy let the anger hang in the air. "At Charlie, and at myself."

Their silence was accompanied by the hum of traffic. Gil checked his odometer. He was going 50 mph.

"Why does Charlie always have to be the one to save the day?

She thinks it's her responsibility to right the wrongs of the world even when it's detrimental to the needs of the people who love her."

"She has a strong commitment to fair play," answered Gil.

"I don't know why I'm complaining to you, Gil. You're just like her," Mandy said with exasperation. "This morning, she was off like Sir Lancelot on a white horse to take care of the guy from last night. She knows I don't want her to do that."

"She knows. But knights see the quest and pursue it."

Gil was still a few blocks away from the Ferry house when Judy called with only a sketchy update on the Hamm search.

"All I know is Charlie called out sick from jury duty, and she and Don went to the Periwinkle house at the crack of dawn. She just called and said they're now on their way to the courthouse."

"So, they plan to confront Goulet at the courthouse?"

"I don't know the details. But Charlie said they didn't find Hamm at his house."

"Okay. Judge Ferry insisted on meeting this morning, but I'll make this appointment as short as possible. Please call me if you hear anything."

Gil was greeted at the door by Brenda Ferry, who was dressed casually in soft-yellow slacks and sweater with matching canvas shoes. She ushered Gil into the house with a face pinched in worry.

"Thanks for coming on such short notice."

"Has something happened?"

"I think you'd better wait and hear it from my husband."

Gil began to turn into the formal parlor where all their other meetings had occurred, but Brenda continued down a hallway to the rear of the house. She paused at heavy double doors and knocked tentatively. When there was no response, she rapped forcefully until the door was yanked open.

Judge Ferry had the annoyed look of being interrupted as he towered in the doorway. His scowl first found his wife, then quickly shifted to Gil. His posture indicated anxiety, and he dismissed the cordiality of hellos. He hurriedly stepped aside and waved his arm to beckon them into the room.

The judge's den was impressive, with pine paneling, built-in bookcases, and a mahogany fireplace surround. Dark-blue drapes had room-darkening backs, and the cloud-soft, wall-to-wall carpeting picked up the blues, maroons, and tan in the room. Coffered beam ceilings carried over to leather visitor chairs and a mahogany desk, behind which a massive desk chair needed only a higher back to become a throne. Ferry slid into the leather seat with easy familiarity and pointed to the guest chairs. He shoved an open law book to the side and placed his forearms on the desk, leaning toward Gil. He was clearly irritated.

"What did you say to my son when you met him last?"

Gil squirmed in his chair. Next to him, Brenda Ferry was as still as a mannequin. The ticking of a corner grandfather clock cast a false calm over the room.

"We talked some about the videos of the assault that showed up on the internet. We spoke about the grand jury process. I coached him through the kinds of questions he might get. I told him the video might not necessarily be introduced by the prosecution because it doesn't really help their case."

"Is that it?" Ferry demanded, in full judicial authority mode.

"That's the bulk of it."

"Did he speak to you about his friends?"

"He spoke of a few friends. Why, what's happened?"

"Jason has informed his attorney that he plans to testify against his codefendants. Did he get that idea from you?"

"No," Gil answered.

"Have you pressured him into supporting that girl?"

"No, I have not, Judge Ferry." Gil leaned forward in the chair. "I don't believe Jason participated in the assault, nor did he do anything to stop it. He feels his own pressure about that."

Ferry could no longer hold back. "Your bleeding-heart stance about that woman, whose own questionable decisions . . ."

Gil stood, about to explode, as Brenda held up her palms in a gesture of peace.

"Your Honor, Maya Hebert was forcibly raped multiple times by multiple men while in an unconscious state." Gil used the formal salutation to warn the judge to stop his interrogation. "There *are* no questionable decisions that would merit that violation," Gil shouted.

The two men tried to stare each other down. Mrs. Ferry fidgeted like she might offer some mediating words, but resettled in her seat. Just then the clock struck the half hour and Gil remembered his goal to keep the meeting short. He put his hands into his pockets and dipped back into his seat.

"Are you concerned Jason's change of heart means he'll have to testify in a public trial?" Gil asked.

Brenda Ferry spoke. "We *were* still hoping to keep Jason from further media scrutiny."

Both men stared at her, waiting for her to say more. When Brenda remained silent, Gil shifted to face the judge, who was staring past his wife toward the fireplace. Gil tried another tack.

"If the prosecutors agree to use Jason as a witness, his charge may be reduced to a misdemeanor or maybe even dropped. They've seen the video footage just like I have. It corroborates Jason's story."

"We know all that. That's not the point."

"What *is* the point?"

Judge Ferry looked at his wife with a gentleness Gil hadn't seen in any of his previous visits. Then he shifted his eyes toward Gil and nestled against the back of his luxurious chair.

"Were you in a fraternity at college?" asked the judge.

"No. I had a basketball scholarship and too many other obligations."

Ferry was surprised. His research on Gil must not have gone beyond his law degree. The judge's arched eyebrows prompted Gil to say more.

"I was an All-City point guard for three years. Then I had a full scholarship at the University of Detroit. I joined the marines after that."

Ferry nodded. His countenance showed new respect for Gil.

"I was never much of an athlete. Jason doesn't get that from me." The judge gave his wife a half-smile. "My wife was a collegiate track star. Made it to the Olympic trials."

"That's impressive," Gil acknowledged.

"I attended a university where my family had a name and a legacy," the judge continued. "I pledged Alpha Phi Alpha. We were all smart, ambitious, studious, with something to prove to the world about black men. We understood the importance of loyalty given and received. Some of those men are still my friends today."

Gil nodded, trying to figure out what was coming.

"How can Jason maintain the respect of his brothers if he shows himself as someone who can't be relied on?"

Gil waited a moment, making sure the question wasn't rhetorical, then said: "Loyalty is important. No doubt about that. But I don't see it as the most important element of a brotherhood. Some people believe in blind loyalty. I don't. People say that justice is blind, and we both know that's not true. I took a vow as a marine to honor my country, and I also served to honor my family. I believe honor is more important than loyalty. Honor isn't blind, Judge Ferry. It's something you do with your eyes wide open. I think Jason just wants to honor you, and himself, by doing the right thing."

"We can see you're an excellent attorney, Mr. Acosta," Brenda Ferry said.

Gil slid behind his steering wheel and reached into his pocket. The note Brenda Ferry had slipped into his hand asked him to meet her at a diner a few miles north on Woodward Avenue.

He pulled into the diner's parking lot and called Judy.

"I'm going to be a bit longer. I'm meeting with Mrs. Ferry separately."

"Is that so," Judy said.

"Any news from Charlie?"

"Not yet."

"Okay, I'll call when I'm on my way to the office."

Gil remained in his car until he saw Brenda Ferry drive into the parking lot. She exited her SUV, nodded at him, and entered the diner. She waved from a booth at the back, and Gil went in and sat across from her.

"Thanks for meeting me. Can I get you something?"

"I'll have a cup of coffee."

"How about a muffin? They have the best."

"Sure," Gil said, unzipping his jacket. "That was a pretty intense meeting at the house."

"My husband has lofty ideas. Now I know you do too."

Gil laughed. "There's quite a bit of loftiness going around the Mack office these days. I'm hoping it won't all bite us in the ass."

Brenda raised her eyebrows, and fiddled with the rolled napkin. The tablecloth was of the red, checkered variety.

"Sorry for the language."

"I've heard worse. Believe me."

The waitress, wearing a pink apron, arrived with an order pad. She looked first to Gil. It was an old-fashioned place. Gil pointed to Brenda, and the waitress didn't register it as a faux pas.

"Two coffees. Two muffins. I'll have a banana nut."

"What kind for you, sir?"

"Do you have a bran muffin?"

Brenda and the waitress smiled simultaneously.

"They have *fifteen* kinds of muffins," Brenda said.

"Wow. What's your most exotic?" Gil beamed at the waitress.

"We have one that's half poppy seed, half blueberry. That's a big seller."

"I'll have that one."

"Okay. Two regular coffees. One Nana. One Bluepoppy. I'll be right back."

Brenda continued toying with the napkin, smiled nervously at Gil, and then set her shoulders. She was the track star going through her routine at the starting blocks. "Mr. Acosta. I want to ask you about Jason."

"Okay."

"Is he, uh, is he all right?"

"I think he'll be fine, Mrs. Ferry. I believe he's been prepped well for his testimony. Whether he testifies for the district attorney or on his own behalf, he'll do fine."

Brenda seemed impatient with Gil's answer. "That's not what I mean. What do you think of him?"

Gil weighed his words. "I think he's a pretty typical twenty-year-old. Because he's an athlete, he's pretty sure of himself. But he's not too cocky. I can tell he's very intelligent, observant, and a bit secretive."

"Is that all?"

"Generally, I think he's a good kid . . . going through what every kid his age goes through. Trying to figure himself out, and his place in the world."

The waitress arrived with the excellent coffee and more-than-excellent muffins. Gil cut his muffin in half to enjoy the mixed-batter pattern, asking "I wonder how they do this?"

"It's pretty easy when you have the right equipment," Brenda said before repeating her starting routine.

"Jason is a lot like his father in many ways."

"And different in some ways, too."

"He never wants to disappoint Bruce. It's difficult for him to defy his father, so it must be very important to him to do what he's doing."

Gil nodded. The next question surprised him.

"Has he told you he's gay?" Brenda asked.

"Yes."

"I thought he might have."

"He didn't offer the information. I found out and asked if it were true. Does his father know?"

"Absolutely not. Bruce is a brilliant man, but on some things his mind is fixed. Jason confided in me that he was attracted to boys when he was about thirteen."

Brenda studied her hands, and twisted her napkin. "He never wants to disappoint his father," she said again.

"Mrs. Ferry, Jason's still grappling with what it means to be gay. He went into a rage when I asked him directly, but later he had a lot of questions."

"You aren't gay, are you?"

"No."

"I didn't think so."

"But I have gay and lesbian friends. There were a few gay men in my unit in Serbia."

"It must have been difficult for them."

"Sometimes. One of them was the best marine I've ever known."

"Bruce thinks there's only one kind of gay man. Weak, flamboyant, effeminate. An embarrassment."

"Jason is very aware of that. He loves his father, but I think he's afraid of him," Gil said.

"Yes," Brenda agreed. "But not physically. He's afraid of the look he'll see in Bruce's eyes when he finds out."

Chapter 16

Wednesday

Charlie and Don sat in Don's Buick, a half-block from the courthouse entrance, with a direct view of Goulet's car and the courthouse. With no hint of Goulet or Hamm at the house on Periwinkle, they'd trekked back downtown and spotted the car parked on St. Antoine.

Don hadn't said much to Charlie during the drive to the house, their examination of the property, or on the ride to the courthouse. Charlie was in assassin mode, so he was being uncharacteristically restrained.

"Think I ought to go inside to see what's happening in the courtroom?" Don asked.

"I guess so. But come right back and let me know."

"Okay."

"If you're not back in ten minutes, I'm coming in."

"If you do, don't forget to leave your gun in the car," Don said. He opened the door to leave, but then closed it and sank back into the driver's seat. "Look, Mack, you're not yourself."

"I'm perfectly fine. I'm just angry."

"You know I've seen you like this before, and you're way beyond angry."

Charlie shot Don a look of annoyance.

"I've got a dog, too, but you can't kill somebody because they hurt your dog."

"Those assholes threatened Mandy. She could have been badly injured. Nobody threatens my family, Don. You'd feel the same way if it was Rita, and don't tell me any different."

"You're not wrong. But I'd expect you to talk me down. And that's exactly what I'm doing for you."

"Go on. Get out. I'll just sit here. I promise. Anyway, I've got to call Mandy."

"Finally," Mandy said. "I've been calling for two hours."

"We didn't find Hamm at Goulet's house."

Mandy's sigh stabbed Charlie in the heart.

"And Goulet?"

"He wasn't there either."

"Charlie, I don't want you to do anything reckless. I mean it."

"Yeah. Okay."

"Don't 'yeah, okay' me."

"What do you want me to say, Mandy? I'm not about to let someone threaten you and get away with it."

"When did you become my protector?"

"I've always been your protector."

"Really. As I recall, it was me that threw her body over yours when a bomb exploded at Cobo Hall."

"Okay. Well . . . we protect each other."

"You want to be everybody's protector. Like one of those Marvel comic superheroes."

"That's not true."

"Isn't it? I could give you a half-dozen examples."

"You're still blaming me for what's happened to Hamm."

"I'm not quite as angry as I was last night."

"What about this morning when you were too tired for a hug before I left?"

"I was still pissed off at you."

"I could tell."

"Well, I'm not anymore. I'm worried. And upset. I'm serious, Charlie. It's not your job to be an avenger. People can take care of themselves, and others will right some wrongs if you just let them."

Don returned to the car at a run, jumping into the driver's seat and slouching. He adjusted the side mirror to see the courthouse steps. Charlie did the same, scooting low in her seat.

"He's coming out now. It must be the lunch break because everybody started pouring out of Courtroom Five."

Charlie peeked over the back of the seat to see Goulet descending the steps. Instead of turning toward them, he turned in the opposite direction.

"He's not going to his car. We need to follow him," Charlie said.

"Come on," Don said, sitting upright and reaching for the door.

"No. Not me. I don't want one of the attorneys or jurors to see me. You go. I'll wait here. Call me when he gets to where he's going."

Charlie continued watching the front entrance of the Frank Murphy Hall of Justice. She'd been so enthusiastic, entering those doors ten days ago to perform her civic duty. Now she felt deflated.

Mandy labeled her obsessive, controlling, and a wannabe superhero. It wasn't the first time she'd heard some variation of those assessments; though she'd always rationalized that her zeal for fairness was a good trait. It was why she'd been attracted to law school, Homeland Security, and now private investigations. From time to time, she might tiptoe through a misdemeanor, or ignore some arbitrary social norm if she felt it harmed an innocent person, but she held a code of honor that sought to find balance in the scales of justice.

Charlie thought she came by it honestly, from parents who would take her along to protests and vigils and marches. She'd been raised hearing accounts of her mother registering Southern voters in the 1960s and about her father's work as a civil liberties attorney. It had been a moral stand when Charlie and Gil left DHS because of the federal agency's profiling policies against Muslims. Don tagged along for more practical reasons, but even he had standards of chivalry when it came to protecting women and children. And control. Well, Charlie's opinion was that without control there would be chaos. Plenty of people had authority, but the real power was with those who controlled resources and information. She understood this at a visceral level.

Charlie's phone rang. She didn't think she could handle another talk with Mandy right now and was relieved when the display identified Don as the caller.

"Quick, drive to the casino. Goulet's waiting around at the valet parking entrance. We may need the car."

Charlie slid into the driver's seat and started the engine. St. Antoine was one-way, and there was too much law enforcement in the vicinity to chance driving the car in reverse four blocks against traffic. She needed to square the block. She headed toward Gratiot Avenue, waiting for a break in the traffic. After a quick scan for police cars, she ran the stoplight and sped toward Beaubien Street, where she had no choice but to wait for a green light. There was plenty of pedestrian traffic but few cars, and Charlie barely slowed at the stop signs as she tore along Beaubien. At the corner of East Lafayette, Don flagged her and hopped in even before the car came to a full stop.

"Turn here and keep going," he ordered.

Charlie sped east, passing the Greektown Casino, as well as the office where the Blue Cross juror worked, and closing in on the Chrysler overpass.

"Did Goulet get picked up?"

"No. He went into the casino."

"Then who the hell are we following?"

"I'm not sure, but Goulet had a conversation with two guys in a dark blue Mercedes."

"The one from last night?"

140

"I hope so. I've been trying to keep up with their brake lights. The car's moving fast, but I think it's only a few blocks ahead of us."

Charlie navigated the Buick at 60 mph, crossing over the I-375 freeway, past Orleans Street, and toward St. Aubin Street. She hadn't had time to adjust the seat and was perched on the edge to reach the pedals.

"Have you ever driven down this way before?" Don asked.

"I'm sure I have, but I can't tell you the last time."

"Wait. Slow down. There he is," Don said pointing ahead at the curb lane.

"Where are they going?"

"We'll soon find out. They're signaling a turn."

Charlie pulled the Buick into the right lane and slowed. The Mercedes turned into the entrance of a housing development. Charlie and Don peered in as they drove past.

"That's the Martin Luther King Apartments," Don announced, unnecessarily since a huge sign identified the complex. "Is there another way in and out of there?"

"I think you can enter from Chene and East Larned streets. What I remember is each entrance is like a cul de sac. Pedestrian sidewalks crisscross the complex, and there's an interior park, but I don't think you can drive through from one end to the other."

"Okay. Go up to the next street, and make a U-turn. Let's switch seats." Don had reverted to his police officer role.

Parked illegally, Don and Charlie stared at the driveway the Mercedes had entered five minutes ago.

"We have to go in there and look for the car," Don said.

"You and I together look like the cops."

"That can't be helped. Let's go."

The driveway led to a parking area. They immediately spotted the Mercedes in the farthest corner of the lot. As Don backed into a space near the entrance, a few pedestrians moved along the sidewalks, but nobody showed any particular interest in the Buick sedan.

"You see anybody in the car?" Charlie asked.

"No."

"I'm getting out to walk around. Maybe I can spot something. You have to stay here."

"Yeah. Yeah, I know. I can't blend in. But those guys might know what you look like. For all we know, they've been in the courtroom, or maybe they have a picture of you."

"They haven't seen me in *this* gear," Charlie said, reaching for her knit cap in the back seat. "You got a clipboard?"

"Under the seat. You doing the meter reader?"

"Yep."

Don reached into the glove compartment and pulled out a plastic card on a chain. "Here, put this on."

"What is it?"

"My firing range ID."

"Great. I guess you don't have a reflecting vest."

"No."

"Remind me to tell Judy we need a few of those."

Charlie clipped her gun to the back of her belt, zipped up a navy quilted vest over her blue hoodie, and let the white badge dangle, photo toward her chest, from the chain around her neck. She grabbed the clipboard and punched keys on her phone until she had the website home page for DTE, the city's energy company, on the screen. She flashed it toward Don.

"Nice touch," he said.

"I'll walk by the car and try to get a look inside, then go up to the houses."

"Be careful."

Charlie walked slowly, but deliberately. Pretending to consult the clipboard, and looking at house numbers, she paused when she reached the Mercedes. She used the clipboard perusal pantomime to sneak a peek inside the empty car. Charlie glanced over her shoulder toward Don, who had rolled down the driver's window. She walked across the grass toward the corner house, and knocked on the door, but there was no answer. She continued from house to house until someone came to the door.

"Can I help you?" an older lady said, peering through the gap in her door. A fat white cat appeared at her feet.

Charlie held out her phone with the DTE logo displayed, and made a show of flashing the ID card. "We have a report of a gas smell. Have you noticed any gas?"

"No. I haven't. Do I need to leave the house?"

"No, ma'am. We're just checking the area."

"Well, you know all our meters are on the side of the end house." She pointed toward the park.

"Yes, ma'am. I'll check that out. Have you noticed any unusual activity in the development?"

"There's always unusual activity. What's that got to do with the gas?"

"Sorry to disturb you. I've only got a couple more houses to check," Charlie said, turning away from the door.

The cat let out a loud and angry yowl.

"That dog barking all night made Fluffy all troubled," the woman said.

Charlie stopped, and turned back to the door. Fluffy purred at the mention of her name, and the lady let the door open wider as she scooped the cat into her arms.

"What did you say about a dog?"

"That no-account man at the corner house got a dog yesterday. We're not supposed to have large pets, but he's always breaking the rules. Anyway, that dog howled and barked on-and-off all last night. Fluffy was very upset. She couldn't even sleep."

Fluffy stared at Charlie indignantly.

"Thank you, ma'am. I'll check the meters."

Charlie stepped down to the walkway, and signaled to Don everything was okay. She retraced her steps to the corner, keeping an eye on the windows at the front of the house. As she rounded the corner house, she spotted a row of utility meters against the back wall. Two first-level windows were a foot above the meters. Charlie glanced at Don again as she was about to move out of his line of sight. She surreptitiously peeked into one of the windows as she crouched in front of the meters. She flipped a page on the clipboard and scribbled on the paper. She was about to move to another meter when the sound of frantic barking made her swivel on her haunches. Streaking toward her from the far end of the community park was Hamm. Charlie leaped to her feet and ran toward him. A man was chasing after Hamm, shouting and swinging a leash.

"Get back here, you mutt," the man screamed.

Charlie sprinted to the parking lot and stopped next to the Mercedes, and Hamm adjusted his angle of escape. He was loping in her direction at high speed. Charlie waved at Don to come.

"What's going on?" a man shouted from the open door of the corner house. He took a step forward, but backed up when he realized he wasn't wearing pants.

Hamm reached Charlie and jumped into her arms, causing her to stagger backwards. Don burned rubber as Charlie lumbered toward the car, carrying the thirty-pound dog.

Just as Don opened the passenger door of the Buick, a bullet ricocheted on the pavement behind her and Charlie dove into the car. The door was still open when Don jammed on the accelerator, sending the car reeling into reverse. Holding Hamm in her left arm, Charlie leaned precariously to grab the car door when a second bullet pinged against the vehicle. Don cursed, swung the Buick into a spin, and careened out the driveway, barely missing a car on East Lafayette.

"Those motherfuckers put a bullet into my car," Don shouted, driving wildly.

Hamm had been licking Charlie's face since he'd jumped into her arms. She held him tight. They were both shivering—Hamm from excitement, Charlie from adrenaline.

"Where are we going?"

"Far away from where we were," Don said, his face lined in concentration.

"We should go to my house."

"Are you sure? That's where they'll probably come looking."

"That's just what I want them to do."

"I thought you were trying to make a good impression in the neighborhood."

"I am."

"So, afternoon gunplay on your lawn probably isn't a good idea."

"Yeah, I suppose."

Charlie was quiet for long time, and Don looked sideways at her. They drove a few more blocks before he interrupted her thoughts.

"You playing with imaginary Post-it notes?"

"Yeah."

"Got any ideas yet?"

"Yeah. I'm calling Mandy."

Chapter 17

Wednesday

Gil left the diner at almost 2 p.m. Mrs. Ferry had made him promise to call or go see Jason again. She wanted him to help the boy with a strategy to come out to his father.

Gil called Charlie as he headed south on Woodward, and she answered on the first ring.

"Gil? What's going on?"

"I'm headed to the office. Where are you?"

"We're all at the office. We got Hamm back."

"You did? Awesome!" Gil paused a moment before asking, "Did you kill anybody?"

"Not yet." Charlie laughed.

Gil listened as Charlie told the story of the pursuit of the dark blue Mercedes, the fake meter reader surveillance, and their harrowing escape. A Grosse Pointe Park police car had been dispatched to Charlie and Mandy's house—a deterrent in case the dognappers showed up again. Mandy and Hamm were safe at the Mack office suite, and Judy was off to find a bone.

"And there's something else, Gil. Don got a call from his sheriff buddy at the courthouse. Remember I mentioned the knitting lady?"

"She's the one who was offered the bribe?"

"Right."

"She was injured this morning in a hit-and-run."

"That's either some kind of bizarre coincidence," Gil said slowly, "or Canova feels threatened. Charlie, these guys mean business."

"I know. So do I."

There was a longer pause before Gil asked, "So, what's phase two in the war plan?"

"We don't have a plan," Don bellowed through the speaker. "And we need one."

Gil's phone beeped with a second call.

"Look, I'll be there in twenty minutes. There's stuff going on with Jason Ferry I need to talk to you about. Don't start planning the next strike until I get there."

Gil hit the flash button on his phone for the incoming call.

"Are you in Detroit?" Detective Holt asked through Gil's car speaker.

"Yep."

"I have two updates."

"Go ahead."

"First, we've turned over all videos to the prosecutors. They weren't happy to get them."

"I bet. They're obliged to disclose the evidence to the grand jury. It could go either way for probable cause, but what's on the footage is consistent with Jason's story. I believe the video evidence actually helps him."

"I do, too. Here's the second thing," Detective Holt said. "Jason called us. He said he knows who raped Maya and will testify for the prosecution."

"I'd heard he was considering that."

"He said he had a talk with you."

"Yes, but . . ."

"He admitted an attorney for one of the boys told him to keep quiet about the rape. The attorney allegedly warned Jason they'd reveal his sexual orientation if he didn't."

"He didn't tell me that." Gil's voice was angry when he added, "I really hope none of the lawyers threatened him."

"Jason's not afraid anymore. He's coming into headquarters this afternoon to fill out an affidavit. He said he didn't trust the campus police. I don't know what you said to him, but it turned him around."

Chapter 18

Wednesday

Luckily, Hamm showed no signs of concussion, mental confusion or physical impairment. Charlie's soreness attested to his running abilities, depth perception, and aim.

"He hit my chest like someone throwing a bag of mulch."

"He's a good boy," Mandy purred, holding Hamm in her lap on the floor. The rest of the Mack team were around the conference table.

Among her other talents, Judy knew just how to care for a canine head wound. Knowledge, she said, which had been acquired over a decade and a half of patching up the abrasions and bruises of her two sons. The tiny scissors in the first-aid kit proved ineffective for trimming the shaggy hair around Hamm's wound, so Judy had Mandy distract him with treats, while she clipped away with a pair from the office supplies. He was content to lie across Mandy's lap for that part of the treatment. Judy cleaned the wound with alcohol and cotton balls, and although Hamm jerked from the sting, he responded to Mandy's baby talk and stayed in her lap. Judy made a trip to the grocery store to purchase spray-on liquid bandage, and with the cut shielded from bacteria, Hamm's good behavior was rewarded with a meaty bone.

Gil lobbed a question at Charlie. "Now that Hamm's back, what's your priority?"

Every time Hamm heard his name he walked over to the person who said it. Gil reached down and gave him a rub behind the ears.

"Well, I've been persuaded, from almost everyone here, to forgo physical violence against Goulet or his goons."

"Unless, of course, they initiate it," Don added. "They're not going to like that you got the better of them and rescued the dog."

"Why not just do what you intended before Hamm was taken?" Mandy said, wrapping her arms around his neck. "You were going to ask for time with the judge to tell her of the jury tampering."

Charlie was nodding in agreement when Gil made an excellent point. "Even with Hamm safe, the threat is still hanging over Charlie."

"You can't be sure of that," Mandy said.

"I'm sorry, Mandy, but these men likely attempted a murder to keep their scheme going," Gil said.

"You mean Mrs. Andrews?" Judy asked.

"Yes."

"You're right, Acosta. These guys aren't going to slink into the night. You've crossed them, Mack, and they're sure to be pissed about that. If you try to shut down this trial, you'll be poking an already angry bear."

"I don't see that I have any choice."

"What would be the best-case scenario?" Gil asked.

Charlie moved to sit on the floor next to Mandy and Hamm. Her partners shifted their chairs to the end of the table to face her.

"I would speak to the judge, and tell her everything I know about the jury. I'd let her know about Goulet showing up in the courtroom and his fugitive status. I'd tell her of the meetings I've witnessed between Goulet and the new prosecutor. I'd tell her of the dinner meeting between Canova, Goulet, and Bateman. I'd tell her about the dognapping, and what we suspect about Mrs. Andrews' hit-and-run."

"Have you really thought through the sequencing? What would happen next?" Gil asked.

"I've thought about it only in general terms," Charlie said, lifting herself from the floor and moving to the whiteboard. "Let's plot it out."

"I can write on the board," Don said, beating Charlie to the marker.

"Fine, Don. Make two columns—one for my actions, the other for the result."

"Good," Gil said.

"Number one: Talk to the judge about the jury tampering. In the other column: Judge investigates, and declares a mistrial."

"Got it," Don said, writing.

"Number two: Share the info we have about Goulet with the judge. And for the other column: Judge has Goulet arrested."

Charlie looked at the board. "Wait a minute. I see what you mean, Gil."

"I thought you would. We have to plot out not only our moves, but Goulet's countermoves, and as many of the unforeseen responses as we can think of."

After a half-hour of mapping actions, Judy left early, and Mandy took Hamm home where the patrol car was still standing guard. In another two hours, Charlie, Don and Gil had devised a plan that generally was the one they'd started with, but this time the moving parts were divided among the Mack Partners. Charlie would still request a meeting with the judge to inform her of the compromised jury. The other notifications—to the Wayne County Prosecutor, and the FBI—were assigned to Gil and Don.

"I've got a few things on the Ferry case I need to discuss," Gil said.

"I'm too exhausted to take in much," Charlie said. "Just give me the highlights."

"The highlights are these: Jason has decided to identify the people he knows were involved in the rape. Judge Ferry is not such an asshole after all. Brenda Ferry already knows Jason is gay, and I promised her I would either call or meet with Jason in the next couple of days to help with his coming out."

Charlie's eyebrows tilted higher with each revelation.

"Don't worry. I'll write it up for you, and everything is in control," Gil said.

"That sounds more like a series of surprises than control. But I trust you. I'll be able to give you some help soon, Gil. Okay, everybody," Charlie said, gathering her belongings. "I'll see you tomorrow, which I predict will prove to be an interesting day. I'm going home to have dinner with my lovely woman and my resilient dog."

Chapter 19

Wednesday Night

Charlie and Mandy cooked pasta and shrimp together, shared a bottle of Riesling, washed the dishes, and then slipped into their coats for an early evening walk. The full moon followed their path, as did the two officers in the Grosse Pointe Park patrol car.

The whole subdivision had been alerted to the assault and dog-napping, and nearby neighbors and other dog-walkers stopped to inquire about Mandy's well being, and to rub Hamm's healing head. He seemed to enjoy being the center of attention, and was clearly happy to be the recipient of the treats neighbors offered from their front steps.

"We live in a good neighborhood," Mandy said.

"We sure do," Charlie agreed.

They waved a goodnight to the officers as they stepped into their front door. Hamm made a dash for the kitchen and his water bowl, and Charlie and Mandy settled onto the living-room couch, cuddling under a flannel throw. Hamm joined them, settling onto his downstairs doggie pallet. After a couple of sitcoms and the local news, they turned off the television and the downstairs lights. Charlie let Hamm out the back door to do his last piece of business for the night, peered out the window to assure herself the patrol car was parked a few doors away, and then secured the house before going upstairs.

"I'm sorry about all this," Charlie said, climbing into bed. "It could all have been avoided if I'd gone to the judge last week."

"Are they out there?"

"Yep. Still there."

"We lose them tomorrow and I'm back to work."

"And it's back to the courthouse for me. To speak to the judge."

"What about the ghost?"

"Don called the FBI tonight to alert them that Goulet's been hanging around the courthouse. He gave them the Periwinkle address and the name of the restaurant where Goulet met Canova and the young prosecuting attorney. Gil's job tomorrow is to talk to his contact in the prosecutor's office."

"So, you each have a piece of the whistle blowing?"

"Yep. We came up with the three-front attack."

Charlie looked across the room where Hamm was sprawled on his giant doggie bed. He looked back at her.

"You think he'll be okay?" Charlie asked. "Maybe he should sleep with us tonight."

Hamm raised his head as if he knew he was being talked about. He wore an expectant look, waiting for an invitation onto the human bed.

"Maybe not tonight. I want to make love," Mandy said, reaching out for Charlie.

"I'm not too obsessive and controlling?"

"You're both. But if you focus it all on me tonight, I'll give you a temporary pass. Turn off the light."

Their lovemaking was languid, intentional, and accompanied by dog snores. Charlie allowed the tension she'd held in her body since yesterday to dissipate into a thick blanket of passion. Mandy was a pliant, receptive, appreciative conspirator in their moonlit dance.

Chapter 20

Thursday

Charlie arrived at Frank Murphy Hall of Justice a few minutes past seven. At that hour there was no line of visitors and no delay in the security check-in. She took the stairs to the second floor and, before entering the jury room, stopped at the clerk's office. The two desks were unoccupied, so Charlie moved to the jury room to drop off her coat. The foreperson, Mr. Naidu, sat at the head of the table reading the newspaper.

"Good morning, Ms. Mack. Are you feeling better?"

"Uh. Yes."

"We missed you yesterday. It was an eventful day."

"Oh?"

"Yes. In addition to your absence, we lost one of our jurors to a tragic accident. Mrs. Andrews was struck by an automobile. She's in critical condition. Our alternates had to fill in for the two of you."

Charlie draped her coat on the back of a chair, looped her backpack on the corner, and sat next to Naidu.

"You don't seem surprised at the news, Ms. Mack."

"I already heard about it. Where is everybody?"

"We didn't have to report today until eight-thirty."

Charlie raised an eyebrow and crossed her arms on the table leaning forward. They were alone, but there were other jury rooms along this corridor, and several people had walked by the open door.

"Mr. Naidu. Someone is tampering with your jury."

"Yes. I know."

"You know?"

"I overheard Mrs. Andrews mention it to you."

"What did you do about it?"

"I reported it to the judge's clerk."

"When was this?"

"Yesterday. After I heard about the hit-and-run accident."

"I have reason to believe several other jury members have either been approached with the promise of monetary bribes, or have already agreed to a bribe."

"To say Mr. Canova is not guilty?"

"Yes."

"Do you have proof of this manipulation?"

"Mrs. Andrews was my proof. But I've identified the person who's coordinating the bribery attempts."

"Mr. Fletcher?"

"No. It's not him, although I'm sure he's one of the compromised jurors, along with three or four others. It's someone who has been visiting the courtroom, off-and-on, throughout the trial."

"I believe the alternate who has taken Mrs. Andrews' seat may also be involved."

Charlie nodded. "What did the clerk say when you reported it to her?"

"She asked if I wanted to speak with the judge about my concerns. I told her yes."

"The judge hasn't requested to see you?"

"No. But that's why I came in early."

"I intended to speak to the judge myself," Charlie explained. "I stopped by the clerk's office on my way in, but no one was there."

"What should we do now, Ms. Mack?"

"Let's go to the clerk's office together and wait."

Charlie and Naidu stood outside the clerk's office fifteen minutes before one of the occupants appeared and entered without a word to them.

"We're waiting for Judge Smoot's clerk," Naidu spoke up after a nudge from Charlie.

"Judge Smoot isn't in yet." The woman glanced up at them momentarily and returned to sifting through forms on her desk.

"I'm the jury foreperson on the Canova trial, and I just need to speak with the clerk."

"I'm not sure where she is, but I can tell her to come find you," the woman said, dismissing them.

Charlie and Naidu returned to their seats in the jury room. They looked toward the door every time someone walked by. The ginger-haired courier came in, followed by his pal. They took seats and continued their conversation about alternative music. It was now eight-fifteen, and jurors arrived in a regular cadence. Fletcher entered the room and nodded to Charlie. Lucy and Pizzemente arrived shortly after and greeted the room. When Trina arrived, she scanned the room and ducked her head when she made eye contact with Charlie. She moved to sit by herself at one of the chairs near the windows. Law student Clint hurried into the room, his backpack bulging. He sat next to Charlie.

"We missed you yesterday," he said.

"Yeah. I had a family emergency."

Trina looked over at them, and then away. Others trickled in, and Naidu counted until they had their full contingent of twelve jurors and one alternate. One of Naidu's duties was to let the clerk know when they had full attendance. He stood, but before he got to the door the clerk walked in.

"Good morning," she recited.

There were murmurs of good morning.

"Okay. We're ready to start. You can form your two lines."

Charlie saw Naidu try to get the clerk's attention and observed how the clerk ignored him. He turned to look at Charlie and shrugged. *What on earth is happening here?* Charlie thought.

In the courtroom, the court reporter and bailiff were in place.

Attorneys at both tables sat examining documents. The gallery was mostly empty except that Goulet was there in the third row. They locked eyes for almost thirty seconds until Goulet gave Charlie a toothy, sneering smile. *You won't be grinning for long, asshole.* Charlie only snapped her attention away from Goulet when she had to stand for the judge's arrival. That's when she noticed the clerk looking her way. *Was everyone involved here? Were they all dirty?*

"Before we begin," the judge said, "I'd like to issue a warning to the jury. It has come to my attention that jurors have been discussing this case among yourselves, as well as outside of the courtroom. You will recall from the orientation video that the effectiveness of the trial system relies on the integrity of the jury. It is one of the most important civic duties you can perform."

The judge took a long pause to scan each member of the jury. Having her stern look fall on you was not a pleasant experience. "This case will draw to a close in a couple of days, and I want to remind the jury there is to be *no* discussion of this case until it is time for deliberations. May I hear your affirmative responses?"

All eyes in the courtroom were on the jury box. Canova leaned over to whisper something in Allan Bateman's ear, and the two prosecutors stared with stern faces. The judge waited until she heard the "yes" of each juror. When it came to Charlie's turn she fought the urge to stand and exclaim her proof of jury tampering. Instead, she complied with the judge's order. She stared at the back of Mr. Naidu's head. He was literally shaking in his seat. Charlie glanced over at Goulet, who was still sneering as if he had just turned over his hole card and it was an ace.

At the lunch break, Charlie walked several blocks away from the courthouse, sat on the curb, and called the office. Judy put her on speakerphone.

"What went on today?" Gil asked excitedly.

"What do you mean?"

"The prosecutor's office is all abuzz about the rogue jury in Courtroom Five."

"The judge admonished all of us for talking about the case. She was pissed. Everyone was shaken up, except Goulet who seemed happy enough."

"Did you speak with the judge?" Judy asked.

"I never got a chance to talk to the judge. The jury foreman and I tried to see her, but we were stonewalled. I think the court clerk is also in cahoots with Goulet. After the judge chastised us, I wasn't sure how to come forward, short of doing that scene from *And Justice for All* where Al Pacino stands and screams that everybody's out of order. I'm sorry for going on and on, but I'm so frustrated."

"Earl Thompson has been fired," Gil announced.

"What?"

"I've been on the phone all day with my friend in the prosecutor's office. Thompson hasn't shown up for work for two days. Nobody's seen him."

"What do you think, Acosta? Did they kill him?" Don asked.

"Killed him, drove him out of town, stashed him away somewhere. I'm telling you, these guys may be amateurs, but that's what makes them so dangerous."

"Getting Thompson out of the way certainly takes care of one of their loose ends," Charlie said. "Don, what did the FBI say about Goulet?"

"They didn't seem at all interested at first. I told them we had information from Homeland Security that laid it all out, and then they started to warm up. They said they'd pick him up."

"Did they say when?"

"You know how the Fibbers work. They never tell you what you want to know."

"So, two out of three of our tactical moves are complete," Gil said. "You still plan to speak with the judge?"

"I'm not sure, Gil. We didn't have a contingency for someone preempting my accusations by distracting the judge with a lesser infraction."

"Maybe you *do* just scream out of order," Gil said. "With everything else that's happened, that'll get you a mistrial."

Charlie chuckled. "Yes. Plus, I'll be tackled by that muscle-bound bailiff, and we'll never have another client again. Look, with the FBI onto Goulet, Thompson out of the picture, and the jury properly warned by the judge, maybe I can just sit tight. I'll call again during the afternoon break."

Mr. Naidu wasn't in the jury room when Charlie returned. A few people sat at the table reading or eating, including Mr. Fletcher. Following the judge's admonishment this morning, nobody was in conversation. Charlie wondered how the judge had become aware of the inappropriate chatter. She moved to the window seat to eat her lunch. She'd finished her sandwich and was sipping coffee when Clint came up to her.

"Got any more of that?" Clint said, nodding at the thermos.

"You're starting to like the hot caffeine, huh?" Charlie asked with a smile.

"It's been a long two weeks."

"You'll get no argument from me on that point."

"The judge was pretty stern this morning."

"Yep," Charlie said, pouring coffee into Clint's waiting cup.

"Did you hear about Mrs. Andrews?"

"Yes. I was very sorry to hear about her accident."

Clint had a strained look on his face and started biting his lip. He leaned toward Charlie to say something when the clerk entered the jury room. She was followed by a red-faced, slump-shouldered Mr. Naidu. Naidu moved to one of the side chairs behind the table.

"I have an announcement. Mr. Naidu will no longer be your jury foreman. Since we're so late in the trial, the judge has selected a replacement, and that is Mr. Fletcher."

Now Charlie was really intrigued. *How the heck does this move fit into the scheme?*

160

Fletcher had been sitting at the table, unusually quiet. He looked up now with a smile as if expecting some applause. One or two people made positive sounds, but the rest just started packing up their lunch remnants and reading material. Charlie tried several times to catch Mr. Naidu's eye, but he wouldn't look at her. The jurors formed two lines and moved solemnly into the courtroom.

Goulet was gone, but Charlie spotted a man and a woman who stood out as FBI agents. Charlie rose, along with the others in the courtroom, as Judge Harrington-Smoot entered and took her seat. The judge announced the defense would wrap up their case that afternoon, and, if time allowed, both the defense and prosecution attorneys would make closing arguments.

Bateman rose from the defense table and called his own client to the witness stand. The move was greeted by a few gasps in the gallery. Prosecutors Spivak and Gleason had a hurried conversation. Gleason began sifting through the documents in her briefcase.

The well-dressed Canova had sat silently at the defense table for the past week and a half, and had not seemed much of an imposing figure. Watching him now as he walked with catlike grace and confidence to the witness box, he exuded the coiled danger that men with power sometimes possessed. Canova's gray tailored suit was one a corporate president might have in his wardrobe. When the equally dapper Allan Bateman stood to question Canova, Charlie thought that rather than a conspiracy trial, she could easily be witnessing a conversation between two Detroit Club acquaintances.

"Please state your name for the record," Bateman began.

"Francis Canova."

"Mr. Canova, do you reside in Detroit?"

"I own a home in Indian Village, but my primary residence is in Huntington Woods."

"Are you married, Mr. Canova?"

"Yes."

"You've heard the testimony of a dozen prosecution witnesses, and I'm going to ask you to clarify and give context to that testimony. Are you able to do that?"

"Yes. To the best of my recollection."

The phrase "to the best of my recollection" became the underpinning of Canova's testimony. He didn't recall sitting next to the city's licensing official on a park bench last spring or having an email conversation with her. He certainly didn't remember giving anything to the manager at the videotaped lunch meeting the FBI had shown to the jury. He also didn't remember giving his accountant any directive that might induce the man to play fast and loose with the company's tax returns. Canova was, however, able to recount what a nice guy he was in giving thousands of dollars in cash to friends, acquaintances, and sometimes strangers who needed a helping hand. He also recalled his humble beginnings as a son born into poverty in an immigrant family that worked hard to make the American dream their reality.

For Charlie, what Canova did or didn't recall became a nonfactor. With every answer his conceit and callousness betrayed his words. Charlie began thinking Canova was better suited to the former Detroit House of Correction than the Detroit Club.

Chapter 21

Thursday

It was time to get a head start on the final report for the Ferry case. Organizing his paperwork chronologically made it clear to Gil this had been a high-touch case, and the Ferrys had been demanding clients from the very beginning.

Charlie had met with the Ferrys for the first time in late August when the second wave of reporting about the fraternity rape case at West Valley University made the Detroit papers. Since then, she'd met with the parents two more times, and Jason twice. She'd interviewed a half-dozen people, including Detective Holt with the Kalamazoo police force, the new chief of campus security, and the lead prosecutor in the U.S. District Attorney's office. Gil had already matched that number of meetings with the Ferrys, Jason, and Detective Holt. He'd also added meetings with Maya and her friends. Now, in addition to his other work, he'd made a promise to Mrs. Ferry to support Jason in coming out to his father. It was a duty that clearly skirted the line between professional courtesy and personal favor.

Gil had left a message for the boy last night, and was relieved when he hadn't called back. He wouldn't have had the energy for a discussion requiring his full emotional presence. But he was surprised he still hadn't heard from Jason, and it was almost three o'clock. He dialed his number, left another message, and then dived into the writing of the final report.

Canova didn't complete his testimony until almost 4 p.m. The judge scanned the jury box and recognized the glazed eyes and weary postures. She banged her gavel.

"Counselors, I don't think it's feasible to get to closing arguments this afternoon. Our jury has not had a break since lunch, and they appear to be worn out. If you have no objections, we'll hold on closing arguments until tomorrow morning."

Neither Spivak nor Bateman objected to the schedule change. The judge turned to the jury. "You are dismissed for the day. Let's reconvene tomorrow morning at 8 a.m."

The once jovial goodbyes and casual conversations among the jurors at the end of the day were nonexistent. Most hurried into the jury room to retrieve their coats and then fled down the narrow hallway that fed into the second-floor corridor.

Charlie took her time putting on her coat and adjusting her scarf. She was looking forward to the walk to the office garage so she could gather her thoughts and reenergize. When she stepped into the corridor, the court clerk stood there, stone-faced.

"Judge Smoot would like to see you," the clerk said.

"Oh, I . . . that's okay. I don't need to see her anymore."

"But *she* needs to see *you*," the clerk responded, handing her a slip of paper. "That's her office number. It's on the third floor."

Charlie tried to read the clerk's expression, hoping it would reveal what trouble she might be in, but the woman was Mount Rushmore.

"Okay. Should I go *now?*"

"She's waiting. You can take the escalator up to three."

Charlie felt the clerk's eyes on her as she rode up the stairs. She checked the piece of paper, looking at office numbers as she walked, stopping at the door with the right number and the judge's nameplate. Charlie knocked, heard a shouted "come in," and entered to find the judge at a large round table directly across from her desk. Also seated at the table were Clint, one of the FBI agents that had been in the courtroom, and the always-sleeping, but now very alert, alternate juror whose name she had never learned.

Gil was busy organizing his report, feeding headings and subheadings into a table of contents template when his office phone rang.

"Judy, do you mind getting that? I'm right in the middle of something," Gil shouted.

Judy walked up to his desk and stared at the notebooks, newspaper articles, typewritten pages, phone messages, and photos strewn on the desk.

"It's Jason Ferry. Do you want to speak with him?"

"Damn. He *would* call now. Yes, I want to speak with him. I wonder why he didn't call on the mobile?"

"He said he did, but you didn't pick up."

"What? Where is my phone?"

Gil patted his jeans pocket, then reached into the pocket of his jacket hanging over the chair.

"Could it be in there?" Judy asked, pointing to the mound on his desk.

Gil used his palm to pat the layers of paper, then lifted a notebook to retrieve his phone. He looked up at Judy, who had her arms crossed.

"You need help with anything?"

"No. I wish. I have to do this myself."

"Okay. Jason's holding on line two."

A minute later, Gil was standing at Judy's desk.

"Jason's coming by. He's in town to see his parents, but I promised his mother I'd speak with him, so . . ."

"So he's coming to get some advice from his new best friend," Judy teased.

Gil ran his fingers through his hair. "How do I get into these things?"

165

"You get into them because you're a nice guy, and you care about people."

"He'll be here in a half-hour. I was hoping to use the conference room. Do you know how long they'll be in there?"

Judy and Gil stared through the glass wall of the conference room where Don and one of the freelancers stood over surveillance photos and phone records. Tamela assisted. They hovered over the table like it was a buffet.

"I don't know. But they've got even more of a paper jungle than you do. So, you better meet Jason somewhere else."

"I wanted to be nearby in case Charlie called. You haven't heard from her?"

"No. But it's almost five, so she should be calling soon."

"Okay, we'll figure it out when Jason gets here."

Clint's eyes bulged like a rabbit's, and he gripped the arms of his chair as Charlie sat next to him. She thought for a moment he was going to reach out to hold her hand. The alternate juror gave her a pleasant smile, the FBI agent stared at her stoically, and the judge cleared her throat.

"Ms. Mack, Mr. Lakeside, thank you for staying to meet with me tonight. Tomorrow I will declare a mistrial in the Francis Canova case. We're aware of the attempted jury tampering, and the FBI is investigating further conspiracy charges against Mr. Canova. Mr. Lakeside, thank you for coming forward last week with your suspicions. Ms. Mack, I know from the FBI and the Wayne County Prosecutor's office that you, or rather your agency, provided information to them about Mr. Canova and some of his associates. Although I'm sure you're aware your behavior as a sitting member of a jury was unorthodox, we believe the information you uncovered will be very helpful to the FBI investigation."

Charlie felt heat climbing up her neck. She couldn't maintain eye contact with the judge, and she joined Clint in gripping the chair. She knew she'd been skating on thin ice with her unautho-

166

rized investigation, and now she was appropriately chastened by the judge's remarks.

"Your Honor, may I ask a question?"

"Of course, Ms. Mack."

"If you've known for a week about the jury tampering, why have you waited to declare a mistrial?"

"That's a very good question. I'll let Agent Percy answer."

Charlie turned toward the FBI agent, but the response came instead from the alternate juror.

"I've been embedded in the jury to keep an eye on the actions of the jurors. We have an ongoing investigation, and I wanted to be sure about each juror's involvement before we shut down the trial."

"What kind of investigation?" Charlie asked.

"This isn't the first time Mr. Canova has been suspected of jury tampering. Nine months ago, a trial on the same conspiracy charges resulted in a hung jury. We suspected an insider was involved in the tampering, so this trial was a way to spring a trap."

"Earl Thompson."

"That's correct," Judge Smoot said.

Clint looked as if he wanted to ask a question, but thought better of it.

"What about Goulet?" Charlie asked.

"Who?" Clint asked.

"That's where your interference caused us problems, Ms. Mack." The stoic FBI agent spoke up. "Mr. Goulet—he no longer goes by that name by the way—works for us. He has for many years."

"But he's doing Canova's dirty work," Charlie protested. "He's been the one meeting with the jurors."

"He was maintaining his cover within the Canova enterprise," Agent Percy said. "I had him testing different jurors. He helped me figure out who could be turned, and who couldn't. I was always listening to the side conversations in the halls and in the jury room."

167

"We all thought you were asleep."

Percy smiled.

"Could you tell us which jurors were involved?" Clint asked.

"Who do *you* think?" Percy asked.

"Mr. Fletcher, the redheaded guy, the bald guy who always sat in the corner, and Trina," Clint said with more than a hint of sadness. "She tried to get me to take some money. I told my father, and he said I should speak to the judge."

"So the corrupted jurors are: Richard Fletcher, Pizzemente, Kelly, Trina Bradley, Lucy . . . the lady who works for the insurance company?" Charlie summed up.

"Lucille Murphy," Agent Percy said. "Very good, Ms. Mack. I see you really put some effort into your very unsanctioned investigation. I watched you working the jury room and taking notes."

"Mr. Naidu?" Clint asked.

"No. He's a straight shooter."

"Then why did you remove him as foreman and give it to Fletcher?" Charlie asked Judge Smoot. "I've never seen a man so dejected. Mr. Naidu was proud to be on jury duty and very proud to serve as the foreman."

"I know. I saw his dejection, too. It was something we had to do to keep Fletcher and the others in tow after my warning to the jury," Judge Smoot explained. "Canova had gotten wind that somebody was snooping about the jury tampering."

"That was probably you," the agent said, looking at Charlie. "Canova was getting antsy, so we came up with the idea of a slap on the wrist about jury chatter. That way Canova could feel secure that his plan wasn't blown, and he was still in a position to buy the not guilty votes."

"What about Mrs. Andrews?" Clint asked. "She couldn't have been involved."

"No," Percy said and shook his head for emphasis.

"Wait a minute," Charlie said. "Wasn't Goulet the one who ordered her hit-and-run?"

"He wasn't involved in that," the agent said. "Some of Mr. Canova's other operatives took that upon themselves. Mrs. Andrews identified the vehicle involved."

"You mean somebody tried to kill her?" Clint's face was drained of blood.

"Was it a Mercedes?"

"How do you know that, Ms. Mack?" the judge asked. "I only have that information because Mrs. Andrews called me from the hospital to report someone had tried to run her over. She thought it had to do with the trial."

"The same guys who drive that Mercedes assaulted my girl-friend, kidnapped my dog, and tried to warn me off my snooping."

"We know about some of that," the agent said.

"I thought those thugs were working for Goulet?"

"No. They take their orders directly from Mr. Canova."

"Well, I know where they live," Charlie said.

"We'd like to have that information," the agent said.

Chapter 22

Thursday

"So, Allan Bateman wasn't involved?" Judy asked.

"I don't know," Charlie said. "I didn't think to ask the judge."

Charlie, Don, and Judy shared a pizza in the conference room. Charlie filled them in on the disclosures from the meeting in the judge's chambers, including the most startling of all: the ghost wasn't the total sleazebag they thought.

"Good thing you didn't get a chance to kick his ass after all, Mack," Don said.

"So tomorrow you're just supposed to show up for jury duty like you don't know anything?" Judy asked.

"Yep. Then the judge will declare a mistrial. I guess the guilty jurors will get arrested or something."

"The FBI will probably swoop up Canova, too," Don said.

"That's very likely. I hope Clint can hold it together. He was badly shaken. Especially when he realized Canova had attempted to kill Mrs. Andrews. I better try to get to him in the morning or he'll blow the whole thing."

They heard a key in the door, and Gil entered the Mack suite and ambled into the conference room. Charlie thought he looked tired.

"You want a slice of pizza, Acosta?" Don asked.

"I just had fried shrimp and fries with the only person I know who could eat you under the table, Don. That boy can surely scarf down some food."

"How is he?" Charlie asked.

"Conflicted, brave, scared."

"But not hungry," Don quipped.

Gil laughed. "No. Not hungry. He *is* going to testify against two of the codefendants. He didn't want to spend the weekend in Kalamazoo because he thinks he'll be harassed."

"He's probably right," Charlie said.

"Did Jason tell his parents what he's going to do?" Judy asked.

"Yes. This afternoon. His father told Jason he'd stand by him if he felt it was the right thing to do."

"That's great. I guess that ends it for us on the case," Charlie said.

"There's one more thing. Jason wants to tell his father he's gay. He was going to do it tonight, but I convinced him to sleep on it. I offered that you and I could meet with him to talk it through."

Charlie glared at Gil.

"Well, I don't know anything about coming out. I don't know if I've been saying the right things to him. He asked me a lot of questions, and I was winging it."

Charlie, still fuming, caught Judy staring at her. "What?"

"You might be able to help the boy."

Charlie was quiet long enough for everyone to know she'd go along with Gil's plan. Gil reached for the pizza box.

"I thought you weren't hungry, Acosta."

"I'm not. Force of habit. I got your text, Charlie. I can't believe Goulet wasn't our guy. I guess you've already gone over the details."

"Yes, but I'll tell them again."

A half hour later all the pizza and soft drinks were gone. Don had already put on his holster and jacket and stood in the doorway.

"So, what did you tell Jason about a time for us to talk?" Charlie asked.

171

"I didn't. I'm supposed to call him," Gil said.

"Since I won't really have jury duty tomorrow, we could make it a Friday lunch meeting. I'll see if Mandy can join us. She knows a lot more about being gay than I do."

"You came out to your mom, didn't you?" Gil asked.

"It wasn't a whole long discussion. I just told her I loved Mandy. You know my mother, she did the research herself."

"Do you know if Jason has someone in his life?" Judy asked.

"I don't think so," Gil said. "He's still confused about what's love and what's just sex."

"Oh geez. I've heard enough," Don said. "Mack, I'll be in the courtroom tomorrow. I've got to see how all this arresting business goes down. Go ahead, keep talking. You guys can figure out this gay stuff without me." Don slammed the door when he left.

Charlie, Mandy and Hamm walked the route they'd taken the night before, but this time without the patrol car following. They bumped into an occasional neighbor, and Hamm was still getting pats on the head and the occasional treat.

"How was it at work today?" Charlie asked. "Are you getting any grief about the incident?"

"No. Everybody's been glad to hear we got Hamm back. I didn't give them all the details. I kind of implied he found his way back to us."

"That's good."

They walked for a while without talking. Hamm revisited the places he'd marked yesterday, and added a fresh layer of possession. It was cold, but there was little wind and the air had the crispness of fall. Some of the houses already had Halloween decorations. Charlie reached for Mandy's ungloved hand, and stuck it in her own pocket to keep it warm.

"I've really taken to heart what you said about my control-freak, avenger thing. Especially the part about how it's important for people to be their own heroes."

"Sitting back is not how you're wired. Neither am I. We both

172

have that first-responder gene. Therapy helped me turn mine down a notch. I know, for example, your mother would like you to worry less about her and give her more room to navigate through the Alzheimer's diagnosis."

"She's told you that?"

"She said she still has her power, and she wants to be able to use it."

Mandy pulled her hand from Charlie's coat pocket and looped her arms around Charlie's waist. They paused for a hug, and Hamm looked back when his leash ran out of slack.

"As it turns out, several members of the jury wanted to make sure Canova didn't have his way. Clint, Mrs. Andrews, and the jury foreman all spoke up. The FBI agent said my snooping almost hindered their investigation," Charlie admitted.

They reached the corner, about to cross the street, when a car pulled to the curb ahead of them. They stopped and Charlie yanked hard on Hamm's leash, watching as the back passenger door flew open. A young woman bounded from the car carrying a bookbag and a gorilla costume draped over her arm.

"Thanks for the ride. See you tomorrow at school," she called out, and waved as the car pulled away from the curb.

She turned toward Charlie and Mandy. Hamm strained to sniff the gorilla suit as she passed. "Hi," the girl said. "Cute dog."

Wordlessly, Charlie and Mandy watched her go up the stairs of the house behind them. Mandy slowly moved her hand away from the back of her jacket. Charlie stared at her.

"You carrying?"

"I think I learned *that* lesson."

"I don't want us to be afraid in our own neighborhood."

"I know. But for a while we'll be cautious. Maybe you were overzealous in your jury service, but you weren't totally wrong. There really were some bad guys."

Chapter 23

Friday

Charlie wore a nice gray pantsuit, her best boots, and a white shirt for her final day of jury duty. Rather than go directly to the jury room, she sat on the opposite side of the corridor pretending to read, keeping her eye on the escalator, the elevator, and the stairwell. She watched a few of her fellow jurors make their way to the jury room. None of them looked her way. She called to Clint when he got off the escalator, and he sat on the bench next to her.

"How are you?"

"I got to tell you, Ms. Mack. That meeting yesterday blew my mind. I told my mother and father about it. I'm really scared."

"You don't need to be. The feds have everything under control now, thanks to you and the others who spoke up."

"And to you. I didn't even know you were suspicious about something going on. You never even hinted."

"I didn't think I should." Charlie touched his arm. "Clint, are you okay about Trina?"

He looked embarrassed, and dropped his gaze. "I thought she was talking to me because she liked me."

"She was definitely flirting with you, Clint. I saw it myself."

"I guess she only wanted to recruit me for Canova."

"She's nobody you want to know. If my suspicions are right, she's the one who got Mrs. Andrews in trouble."

Clint gripped his knees tightly.

"She's bad news. But you couldn't have known that. Look, don't talk to anybody when we get to the jury room. Just say hello and act naturally; get one of your books out and start reading. We better get in there. Judge Smoot said we'd be called into the courtroom right away."

As promised, the court clerk came for the jurors promptly at eight. Richard Fletcher nodded to Charlie with a smile, and he lined up in front of her. Charlie watched Clint's shoulders stiffen as he took his place in line. She managed to catch Mr. Naidu's eye and smiled. He gave her a sorrowful look.

Spivak and Gleason stared at the jury as they filed into the courtroom. Charlie noticed Ms. Gleason's bulging briefcase was missing from its usual place on the table. Bateman and Canova huddled, looking up briefly, but continued with their whispered conversation. The bailiff sat in his usual place, but a second sheriff stood near the main door.

The gallery had the usual dozen or so visitors. Don positioned himself in the center of the third row and gave Charlie an almost imperceptible nod. Yesterday's FBI agent sat with another agent in the row behind Don. Charlie didn't immediately recognize the thin African-American man slumped in the last row of the gallery, but then her spine stiffened. It was Hamm's abductor. Charlie's heart raced. She'd given a description of this man and his friend to the agent in Judge Smoot's chamber along with the location of their house at the MLK Apartments. Obviously he hadn't been captured. She tried getting Don's attention, but he was staring at the back of Canova's head. Charlie had no idea how this was all going to go down, but seeing the man again who had threatened Mandy and taken her dog made her feel tense and worried.

The clerk took note of Goulet's late arrival, which also elicited a shifting of the chairs in the jury box. Goulet sat on the end seat in the last row, glanced quickly at the jury box, then focused on the front of the room. The clerk rose from her seat, directing everyone else to follow suit, as Judge Harrington-Smoot entered the courtroom from the door behind her bench.

Smoot wore a very somber expression as she adjusted herself in her chair and placed her gavel in front of her. She glanced first at the sheriff at the rear of the courtroom and then turned to the jury.

"Unfortunately, ladies and gentlemen of the jury, I must declare a mistrial in the case, *The State v. Canova*. Your services are no longer needed. Court is adjourned."

There was a stunned silence in the courtroom. A commotion finally began at the defense table when Allan Bateman almost knocked over his chair as he stood, shouting "Your Honor?" Canova rose next to him, red-faced and double-fisted. The bailiff moved to stand in front of the bench, and crossed his bulging arms.

Without another word Smoot gathered her papers and gavel, the clerk ordered the courtroom to stand, and the judge departed. The two FBI agents moved toward Canova. Goulet got up quietly, and the officer at the door stepped aside as he exited. The clerk approached the jurors, directing them to return to the jury room. As she left the courtroom, Charlie looked back to see the agent from last night's meeting place a restraining hand on Canova's shoulder while the other agent wielded handcuffs. Charlie had only a moment to catch a glimpse of Don, who faced the rear of the courtroom. The skinny thug had blended in with the other courtroom observers departing through the main door. *Dammit!*

Charlie stepped into the jury room where she found confusion and raised voices. The court clerk closed the door and placed herself in front of it. Charlie took a seat.

"What the hell is going on?" Richard Fletcher demanded of the clerk. He looked intimidating as he stood over her.

"You'll be able to leave in a few minutes," the clerk said, holding her ground, not flinching.

Charlie had been very wrong about her.

"What happened in there?" Mr. Naidu asked, standing next to Charlie.

Charlie shook her head and tugged him into the chair next to hers as Clint came over to sit on her other side. The alternate juror-slash-undercover agent stayed near the front of the table.

Charlie looked up to see Trina eyeing her and Clint. Lucille, the insurance lady, and Mr. Pizzemente stood at the other end of the room watching Fletcher. They all looked trapped.

The sharp knock at the door quieted everyone. The court clerk inched the door ajar and then swung it open to the bailiff and two Wayne County sheriffs.

First, the clerk pointed to Mr. Fletcher.

"That one. Those two," she said in the direction of Pizzemente and Lucille. "Her," she said pointing at Trina. "Him," the clerk said, indicating Kelly. The ginger-haired courier was asked to stand by one of the sheriffs. "And him," the clerk made a special point of tilting her head at the undercover agent-alternate.

The remaining jurors held their breath as the six were escorted by the sheriffs out of the room. The clerk closed the door behind them with a heavy clunk.

"You will be paid for today. Checks for your jury service should arrive within a week. You can go now, and thank you for your service. Please leave in an orderly manner."

The "I'm done" look on the clerk's face shut down any questions. She waited at the door as the jurors, still stunned by the morning's events, moved lethargically, gathering their belongings. She nodded to each person as they exited. She gave Charlie and Clint a curt smile as they passed. "Thank you, Mr. Naidu," Charlie heard the clerk say as he brought up the rear.

The group of blameless jurors gathered in a circle on the sidewalk to ask questions about what just happened. Charlie let the others talk.

"Did you know about this?" the man who had become Kelly's new pal asked Mr. Naidu. "I didn't have a clue. I kind of feel betrayed."

"I didn't know this would happen today," Naidu said, "but I did report my suspicions of wrongdoing to the clerk." Mr. Naidu's shoulders were noticeably straight again.

"I did too," Clint offered.

Charlie could see him feeling good about his insider status, and he was about to say more, but she stopped him with a look.

"The whole trial felt jinxed," the real alternate juror said. "Especially after what happened to that old lady. You know, the one who was hit by a car?"

The small group offered noncommittal murmurs to his idea. There were a couple more questions, then the awkwardness of strangers making small talk kicked in.

"Well, I'm out of here," the alternate said. "Good luck to you all."

The rest of the group dispersed, leaving Charlie, Clint and Mr. Naidu. Charlie saw Don's car up the street.

"Ms. Mack, it was nice to meet you," Naidu said. "You too, young man."

Charlie and Clint responded in kind.

"Thank you, Mr. Naidu. You were a great foreman," Charlie said as he nodded and walked away with the stride of a proud man.

"Jury duty was much more eventful than I'd imagined," Clint said, extending his hand. "Thank you for the support and the coffee."

Charlie brushed his hand aside and kissed him on the cheek.

"I know you will become an impressive lawyer. Or maybe an impressive musician."

They both laughed. Charlie gave him her business card, adding, "Whatever you decide, I know you'll do well."

"Are we going to the office?" Don asked, starting the Buick. It was just nine o'clock.

"Yeah. Gil and Judy aren't going to believe it."

"I gotta tell you, Mack. I've never seen anything like that."

"What happened after I left the courtroom?"

"They cleared the room and then perp-walked Canova out into the corridor. He was yelling at Bateman all the way. He made so much noise bailiffs came out of the other courtrooms. There's a press room at the end of the hall, and a couple of reporters came out at a run. An FBI agent and a sheriff escorted Canova down the stairs and out of the building. I'm pretty sure Bateman wasn't part of the scheme. He looked too dumbfounded."

"What about the guy who snatched Hamm?" Charlie asked.

"What about him?"

"Didn't you see him? He was in the courtroom, sitting in the back."

Don shook his head. "Nope. I didn't know he was there."

"I looked back at you as they herded me into the jury room, and I thought you had eyes on him."

"Damn. Sorry. With all the confusion I didn't even notice him. How could he be there? I thought you told the FBI where to find those guys."

"I did."

Gil took a break from writing the Ferry final report to join Charlie and Don at Judy's desk as they provided accounts of the courthouse drama. Don described in detail the confusion in the gallery after the judge gaveled the trial closed. He'd seen Canova snatched away from a few reporters and then hustled into a ground floor office used by the county sheriffs. Don's sheriff buddy had allowed him into the room just in time to see the black police SUV, pulsing red-and-blue lights, carry Canova away onto Raynor Street behind Frank Murphy Hall of Justice.

"They're already reporting about it on WWJ radio," Judy said.

"It's hard to keep something like that away from the media too long. My buddy said they were alerted this morning to have extra sheriffs on hand," Don said. "The district attorney's office and the FBI informed them a couple of days ago that something was going down today."

"So that's why Spivak and Gleason didn't seem surprised," Charlie said.

"Don, did your guy know anything more about Thompson?" Gil asked.

"Oh yeah. I forgot to mention that. We were wrong about Thompson being bumped off by Canova. The FBI has him," Don said. "He cut some kind of deal. He's been assuring Canova that everything was still all right and that he'd get either a hung jury or a not guilty decision."

The Mack partners listened open-mouthed as Charlie recounted the final tense scene in the jury room. Judy smiled as Charlie described the actions of the clerk, and Gil nodded when Charlie speculated that the removal of the planted FBI agent was to maintain his undercover status.

"Did everyone go quietly?" Don asked.

"I think Trina caused the biggest scene. The Fashionista girl," Charlie said in response to the question mark on Gil's face. "I know. It was hard to keep up with all the names."

"What did she do, break a nail?" Judy wisecracked.

"No, but she tried to shake the bailiff's hand off her arm, and acted like a prima donna, so she was handcuffed. She was a snappy dresser, but not a nice person. Clint had a crush on her, so I think having that last memory of her will help him get over it fast. Now that everything is over, the thing I feel best about is how Mr. Naidu and Clint acted to do the right thing."

"I hear you and Mandy have been talking things through," Judy said, smiling.

Charlie gave her a questioning look.

"I called her to check on Hamm," Judy explained.

"We have. She gave me some things to think about. Why didn't you all try to talk me down?"

Don, Gil and Judy stared at her with an astonishment that said it all. Even the temporary assistant, Tamela, glanced up from her task. She quickly looked away, but not before Charlie saw the beginnings of an eye-roll.

Chapter 24

Friday

Charlie had gotten home by eleven and prepared a large bowl of tuna salad with all her favorite ingredients: mayo, diced egg, pimiento olives, red onions, celery, and relish. Hamm monitored her work. A bowl of potato chips and a plate of wheat crackers were already on the dining table. She was spinning salad greens at the kitchen counter when Mandy came through the front door, greeted Hamm, and hung her holster on the clothes tree. Charlie met her in the vestibule for a welcome home kiss.

Mandy still had a small bruise on her left cheek, and a few scrapes on her hands that hadn't quite healed, but she was otherwise her normal gorgeous self. Her thick red hair was always tied up in a band when she was on duty, but in her well-fitting, tan and dark brown uniform, she still looked like a model in a police recruitment ad.

"Do I have time to change?"

"Aren't you going back to work?"

"No. I took a half-day."

"Gil and Jason should be here any minute, so if you wouldn't mind could you just wash your hands and slice some tomatoes to garnish the plates?"

Mandy appraised the table as she passed through the dining room, then stopped at the counter where Charlie was layering greens on four dinner plates.

"What did you make?"

"Tuna salad."

Mandy was motionless for a moment, then moved to the refrigerator, grabbed a package from the meat drawer, and turned on the stove's broiler.

"What are you doing?"

"Cooking some bratwurst. You are not going to feed tuna salad to a twenty-year-old boy in my house."

"Why?"

"He won't like it."

"But I put all the good stuff in it. Olives, relish, egg."

"Did you put chunks of beef or pizza in it? If you didn't, he's not going to like it."

"So, you know this how? Wait, don't say it. Because you had a brother and I didn't."

Mandy placed two brats on the broiling pan.

"I hate cleaning that pan," Charlie complained.

"You won't have to do it. I will."

"Do we have any baked beans?" Mandy asked, rummaging through the cupboards. "Some frozen French fries?"

"No."

"Well, the chips will have to do. Oh, but we do have pretzels."

Mandy added the pretzel bowl and jars of mustard and ketchup on the table. Charlie selected place mats and napkins from the sideboard.

"Are you going to change clothes?" Charlie asked.

"I need to stand by the stove and watch those brats," Mandy replied. "The broiler's on the highest setting."

Hamm's hopping and barking at the front door signaled Gil and Jason's arrival.

"They're here," Charlie yelled over her shoulder and moved to the front door. Hamm was so excited she had to grab him by the

182

collar to yank him away from the door. "It's okay, boy. We have a new visitor, and Gil. You know Gil."

Charlie opened the door with a smile and pulled Hamm back a half step. But it wasn't Gil and Jason at her threshold; it was Mandy's skinny assailant. He stepped through the door with a Taser, and fired it at Hamm. Charlie cried out as a second man, the one Charlie had last seen without pants at the MLK apartments, pushed the barrel of a gun into her gut. Charlie's shout and Hamm's yelp brought Mandy running to the front of the house. Now the skinny man also brandished a gun, and he pointed it at Mandy, bringing her to an abrupt stop. Mandy looked at Hamm trembling on the floor, and prepared to charge the skinny man.

"Don't be foolish, lady," the bigger guy said. "I'll kill you before you even get near that dog. Sit down," he ordered. He pointed the gun at Charlie's head. "You too."

Charlie reached back for Mandy's hand and shifted away from the door. "Do what he says, Honey."

"So, you two really are, like, dykes. I didn't believe it when Mr. C told me. Two good- looking women like you."

The man's eyes narrowed, an idea forming, as he looked between Charlie and Mandy.

"If my dog dies, I'll kill you," Charlie said.

The man coughed a laugh. "That's funny, because I plan on killing you. You've been nothing but trouble to me and my livelihood. Because of you, I don't have a job, and I have to get out of town. So, I'm going to rob you and then kill you."

"You didn't say anything about killing anybody, Raymond," the skinny guy said in a weak voice.

"Shut up, man. Go get two chairs and find something to tie these bitches with."

Charlie held onto Mandy's hand and squeezed it to signal *stay calm.* Mandy squeezed back. Hamm was still down and unmoving, but he was breathing steadily. The man called Raymond took a few steps into the living room. He looked at the TV and the Bose speaker system. He picked up the silver picture frame with the photo of Charlie's father and mother.

"You got some nice stuff here," he said as if he were an invited guest or an antiques appraiser. Then he shouted toward the rear of the house. "You find anything yet to tie them up?"

"Not yet. I'm looking under the sink for some twist ties."

Charlie's backpack was on the coffee table, and Raymond picked it up. Keeping his gun pointed toward them, he unzipped it and lifted out her laptop and purse. "Oh yeah. Now we're talking."

Charlie tapped Mandy's palm and nodded to her gun holster on the clothes tree. Mandy returned the tap.

Raymond was using both hands now to get into Charlie's wallet. Charlie heard a car pull into the driveway, but so did Raymond. He dropped the wallet and ran to the window. Suddenly, the burning bratwurst caused the smoke alarm's shrill scream to fill the house. Raymond, startled, turned toward the kitchen. In one swift move, Charlie lifted from the floor and flung herself at the man, tackling him at the waist. He fell hard on his face, and his gun skittered under the dining table. Raymond kicked at Charlie, but pinning his hand in a painful position, she flipped him over and expertly looped her arm around his neck.

The skinny man sprinted into the dining room, but realizing his gun was still in the kitchen, he sprinted back. Instead of retrieving his pistol he fumbled with the back door until he flung it open. When Mandy's bullet whizzed over his shoulder, he stopped, turned, and raised his hands in surrender.

At the sound of the gunshot, Jason and Gil, who had been pounding the front door, crashed through it like the offensive line of the Detroit Lions. They skidded on the broken door and landed in a heap on the foyer floor. With both front and back doors now open, the screeching smoke alarm finally fell silent.

Sprawled on the dining-room floor, Charlie held Raymond in a rear choke hold, her legs wrapped tightly around his torso. He was fifty pounds heavier, but they were equal in height, and he was losing oxygen. He flailed hard. His elbows pounded into

Charlie's sides, and he pulled at her arms. He reached up to grab her head, but she evaded his efforts. In about fifteen seconds his legs began to quiet, and he could only slap at Charlie's arms around his neck.

"Stop, Charlie, you're killing him," Gil shouted, leaning over them.

"I told him I would."

The terrifying calmness of her own voice snapped Charlie back to awareness. Only then did she stop resisting Gil's efforts to pry her arms and legs away from the unconscious man.

In the kitchen, the skinny man lay facedown. Mandy had retrieved his gun from the sink and turned off the stove. Her own gun drawn, she squatted next to him.

"Are you the one who hit my dog in the head?"

"I didn't mean to hurt him, lady, uh, officer. I just wanted him to stop coming at me."

"And you didn't mean to tase him either. Put your arms behind your back."

Mandy handcuffed the man to the refrigerator door and went to check on Charlie, who sat against the dining-room wall, knees lifted and head buried in her folded arms. Gil stood over the revived Raymond, and signaled to Mandy that Charlie was all right. Then Mandy rushed to the foyer where she saw Hamm cradled on Jason's lap. The dog's body still trembled from the tasing, but he wagged his tail twice when Mandy said his name. Jason looked at Mandy, wide-eyed and ashen.

"Hi," she said, sitting next to him on the floor. "I'm Mandy. Welcome to our home."

A Detroit police crime unit remained at the house three hours collecting guns, assailants, and explanations. The Grosse Pointe Park police stayed an additional hour to make sure their own officer was okay and had provided a full account of the discharge of her firearm. Don and Judy wanted to rush over, but Charlie assured them that she, Mandy, Hamm, Gil and

Jason were all right, and they should keep doing the work of the office. Don said he'd check with the police and FBI to find out what he could about Canova's role, if any, in the home invasion.

Gil supervised the three-person locksmith crew who resecured the front door frame and put a new lock on the scraped, but intact, door. The cut-out panes were temporarily replaced with plexiglass.

Jason *did* like tuna salad. He ate two plates, all the chips, a lot of the pretzels, and a pitcher of lemonade. Hamm got a special one-time treat of a tiny bit of heavily charred bratwurst. Hamm and Jason had become buddies, and while Charlie, Mandy, and Gil answered the questions of police and a few neighbors, the two retreated to the quiet of the basement where Hamm got cuddles and treats, and Jason watched TV.

When Charlie, Mandy, and Gil finally made their way to the basement sanctuary, Jason and Hamm were both rolled up on the couch asleep.

"I'm sorry this turned out to be so . . . so crazy," Charlie said, after shaking Jason awake.

"So, are you some kind of ninja badass?" Jason asked.

"I'm not too proud of what happened. I lost my head," Charlie said apologetically.

". . . and she has a couple of black belts," Gil said. "And has studied a few different martial art forms. So, she *is* a ninja badass."

"Wow," was all Jason managed to say.

"So, young man," Mandy spoke up. Then realized she sounded like her father, and started over. "Jason, I'd hoped to meet you under calmer circumstances. Gil said you wanted to talk to Charlie and me."

Jason looked at Gil, ducked his head, and reached over to rub Hamm, who sat next to Mandy's leg. Gil had described him as a confident, almost cocky, young college man who had grown up in privilege and high expectations. Right now, with his socks off, and sleep still in his eyes, he looked like Mr. and Mrs. Ferry's little boy.

"Yes, ma'am. I'd like to talk to you and Ms. Mack about . . . about what it's like being gay."

"Well, first of all, please don't call me ma'am. I haven't had time to take off my uniform, but here we're just people like you."

Hamm jumped on the couch next to Jason, requesting to be petted, which seemed to free Jason to speak. He told them he had known about his attraction to other boys when he was a young teen. His mother hadn't made him ashamed of those feelings, but had warned he shouldn't tell his father. Although Jason and his father were close, that secret had stood between them for seven years. He had faked his way as a ladies' man through high school, but in college, had begun to explore his feelings and urges away from campus. He thought nobody knew about his sexuality, but after his arrest for the Maya Hebert assault, his secret had caught up with him.

"It's the main reason I didn't speak up before now. It wasn't so much that it would affect me at school. I don't care about that so much anymore. I've even thought about transferring to another college. I have friends in Grand Rapids who lead their lives as openly gay men. I think I really want that for myself, but it would embarrass Dad."

"Are you very sure about that?" Mandy asked.

Jason glanced at Charlie. "I know my father."

"I came out to the world when I was in high school," Mandy said. "My parents were great about it, but I know that's not everyone's experience."

"No, it's not," Charlie said.

"Charlie and I have talked about the difference for blacks and whites when it comes to being gay or lesbian. She's told me it's harder because it's still true that being black in America already comes with burdens."

Jason's eyes lit up with the appreciation of being understood. "That's it, exactly. Dad always told me I had a lot to prove as a black man. He and his friends still talk about it all the time. He cares, a lot, what people think of him . . . and his family."

"I never really came out," Charlie said. "I had male and female sex partners, starting in high school. My father died when I was twelve, and my mother and I never really talked about those kinds of things."

"So, are you bisexual?" Jason asked.

"I don't really do the labels. I've been married before—to a very nice guy—but I wasn't happy. I know that I love Mandy. That's what I told my mother, but it wasn't easy for her to understand at first."

"So how did you get her to understand?"

The questions, answers, and personal anecdotes went on for three hours. Mandy changed her uniform and put more bratwurst in the broiler. This time they didn't burn, and Hamm didn't get a sample. Charlie pulled four beers from the small refrigerator by the bar, and they talked while they ate.

At eight o'clock Gil drove Jason home, and Charlie and Mandy moved through the house, cleaning up and discussing the harrowing day they'd been through.

"Tomorrow I'm mopping the kitchen, foyer, and dining room with bleach," Charlie said.

"Purging the danger and bad vibes?"

"Something like that."

"We have the whole weekend to reclaim our space. It began tonight with the chance to talk to Jason. It was good to eat and drink a beer with friends. To do something normal in our home on the same day something so abnormal occurred."

"I almost killed that guy," Charlie said quietly. "If Gil hadn't stopped me, he'd be dead."

"Not that he didn't deserve it, but I'm grateful you didn't. Are your ribs still sore?"

"They'll be sore for a few days, and he scratched up my arms pretty good, too. The asshole. I'm surprised you didn't pistol-whip that skinny guy. You were ready to take him down when he had the Taser."

"It had something to do with being in uniform. I really wanted to hurt him for hurting Hamm. I would have too if I had been just Mandy Porter, citizen."

"You think the neighbors want us to move?"

"No. I spoke with the guy next door. He saw Gil and Jason crash through the door, and he heard the smoke alarm. At first, he thought the house was on fire. I explained that we managed to find the guys who attacked me and Hamm. He was happy about that. It's fortunate that on a weekday at noon most of our neighbors are still at work."

"So, we can stay?"

"For the time being. Ready to go upstairs?"

"I guess so."

"I think I'll sleep good tonight."

"I hope I can," Charlie said.

Chapter 25

On the Tuesday following Charlie's jury duty, Jason's grand jury appearance, and the traumatic home invasion, things were slowly getting back to normal in the Mack offices. Judy checked the file folders the temp had organized. Charlie sat at her desk returning a week's worth of phone calls, and Don cleaned his gun. Gil was back from a trip to Kalamazoo—a final time to give support to Mr. and Mrs. Ferry and Jason, whose grand jury testimony had resulted in the indictment of four members of the Gamma squared fraternity. Jason's misdemeanor charge had been dropped, but he would have to testify in several more trials.

The Mack partner meetings happened once a month, and Judy always brought in Danish, fruit, and juice. In those meetings Charlie, Don, Gil and Judy discussed the status of the agency's coffers, and did long-term planning. But the updates on cases, clients, and personal issues were a higher priority than the strategy conversation today. Charlie began with a report on her house and neighborhood.

"Our door's been professionally repaired, and it was Mandy's idea to get a company in to do a deep-clean of the downstairs. They even cleaned the stove. So, we feel like it's our house again."

"How's your dog?" Gil asked.

"We took him to the vet on Saturday, just to get him checked out. He's fine. By the way, the vet said you did a great job on his head wound, Judy."

"The neighborhood watch committee hasn't come by to ask you guys to move?" Don joked.

"Thankfully, no. But I told Mandy it would be good for us to be as normal as possible for the rest of the year. So, to help, we went out and bought about a hundred dollars' worth of Halloween candy for tonight. The good stuff. We also put some cool decorations on the porch."

"I got a call this morning from my contact at the sheriff's office," Don said. "Your two bad guys are being transferred to a federal prison. They have the local charges of home invasion and assault, but the FBI wants them for a bunch of other things related to Canova's activities over the past year. Apparently, they have a witness who gave them all the information they need."

"That's probably Caspar the ghost," Charlie said. "Clint called to say he'd visited Mrs. Andrews in the hospital. She's getting rehab for a broken femur, but otherwise she's going to be all right."

"Has anyone heard anything about that young prosecutor, uh, Thompson? After I did all that research on him I feel like I know him," Judy said.

"I haven't heard anything," Gil said. "But he made his own bed. Goulet will probably have plenty to report about him, too."

"Despite all that happened, I'm glad I served on jury duty. It taught me a lot about myself, and about the relative decency of people. For every one of those bad guys, there was a person, or two, or three, trying to do the right thing."

"Like you," Judy said.

"Thanks, Judy. Yeah, like me. But also Clint, and Mr. Naidu, Mrs. Andrews . . ."

"And don't forget Jason," Gil added.

"Right."

"We're done now with the Ferry case?" Judy asked.

"We're done," Gil said. "I finished the report over the weekend and drove to the Ferry's on Sunday. I took the invoice too. I sort of wanted to check on Jason."

"Has he spoken to his father yet, about . . ." Charlie began.

191

"Not yet. But I know he will. I had lunch with them after Jason's testimony. He's transferring to another school with his father's blessing. So, I know everything will work out for them in the end. Mrs. Ferry and Jason will win the judge over."

"I'm glad to hear that," Charlie said. "He's a good kid. I trust anybody that Hamm trusts."

"By the way, here's our final payment," Gil said, sliding a check to Judy.

Don ended the updates with a summary of the surveillance cases. Two more had been added to the roster, and despite Charlie's disdain for such investigations she admitted being ready for a few simple cheating-spouse cases.

Charlie and Judy reported on the agency's cash flow, which, with the Ferry payment, was on solid footing. In the next few months they had work from the Wayne County Supervisor's office and Wayne State University. They were also being hired as subcontractors on a security detail for a visiting head of state coming to January's North American International Auto Show.

"That will bring us full circle during the last two years with another presence at the auto show," Don noted.

"Right. So, this would be a good time to map out next year. Set some benchmarks for ourselves. Maybe block in vacation time if any of us have some planned," Charlie said.

"Well you can block me out for May. That's when our baby girl is due," Don said.

"It's a girl?" Charlie asked, grinning.

"Yes, Rita finally agreed to an ultrasound, and everything looks good."

Don smiled like a man who had won the lottery. He accepted a hug from Charlie and a high-five from Judy. He reached across the table to accept Gil's handshake.

"I'm happy for you, Don," Gil said.

"Thanks, partner. It feels good. Rudy's very excited about his baby sister."

"I have some good news, too," Gil said. "It's mostly good."

Don reached for a Danish, and Judy filled her coffee cup.

Charlie stared at Gil, looking for a hint of his news. She felt a sick feeling in her stomach.

"Darla and I are getting married."

The conference room erupted in celebration. Don rose to circle the table and patted Gil's back so vigorously he began ducking the blows. Judy and Charlie stood by, waiting to give hugs and kisses. Don poured juice and offered a toast: "To our long-lost bachelor. Marriage couldn't happen to a better guy."

"Darla must be ecstatic," Charlie said.

"Yes. She's very, very happy. So am I." Gil smiled broadly. "The other news is Darla has a new job. It's one she's been waiting for."

"That's great, Gil," Judy said.

"But, there's something else, isn't there?" Charlie said, her disquiet rising.

Gil's mouth tightened, and he closed his eyes for a second.

"Darla found a job in Washington, DC. So, we're moving to Washington in early January."

Charlie and Mandy were propped up in bed with Hamm at the foot where he'd been starting off the nights since being tased. He usually got up after a couple of hours to curl up on his own bed. Mandy had been worried about him tonight with the dozens and dozens of strangers coming to the door for trick-or-treating, but he loved kids, and within a half-hour the sounds of footsteps on the porch didn't send him into a panic. They had only a couple of bags of candy left over, and from the impromptu reviews from kids and parents, their house had the best candy on the block. They were finally relaxing and catching up on the day.

"You told me after the Corridor case, with all the emotional trauma he suffered, that Gil might leave the agency," Mandy said.

"I know. But, when it didn't happen right away, well, I wasn't prepared for it now. I've come to rely on him too much."

"How did Don and Judy take the news?"

"You know Don. He tried to be stoic, but I know how much

he likes Gil. He doesn't get along with everybody—not even Gil sometimes—but he trusts Gil. Judy broke down and cried. It took Gil fifteen minutes to console her."

"When's he leaving?"

"He's going to work full-time through next month; then he needs to work part-time because he and Darla have to find a house in DC."

"Are they getting married in DC?"

"No. They're getting married right away. In the next few weeks. We'll get an invitation." Charlie put her book down and pulled her knees up to her chest. "Everything's happening so fast."

"You're going to need to hire somebody else."

"I can't even think of that. Unless you want to quit your job and come work with us."

"I don't think that's a good idea."

"Why not?"

"Working together and living together might put a strain on our relationship. We'd rarely have time to be our individual selves. Besides, that would make you my boss, wouldn't it?"

"I already thought I was the boss."

"In your dreams."

They laughed, and Hamm walked up the bed to get some of the kissing that was going on. Finally, Charlie shooed him to the floor.

"Okay, buddy, time for you to get in your own bed."

He stared at her to be sure she meant it, then bounded off the human bed and plopped onto his doggy sleeping couch. Charlie and Mandy watched him fight to stay awake, and then with a deep sigh fall to sleep to the sounds of his own snores.

"I guess I will have to hire someone. Don and I work well together, but I need another attorney in the office. Someone who can take on the filings and help with court briefs and client depositions."

"You could do that yourself. What percentage of the work is it? Ten percent, fifteen?"

"This year it was close to twenty percent of our work."

"That doesn't sound like so much time that you need an attorney. What about the other stuff Gil does? The special forces stuff. That's come in handy from time to time. And his charm skills. That's the stuff you're going to miss."

"You're right, and you're killing me. I'm never going to find anyone to replace Gil. The three of us, plus Judy, worked so well together."

"Don't worry about it tonight. You've got more than a month to figure it out. Gil will help you."

"That's the other thing I'll miss. His brain. He was always the one asking the theoretical questions, bringing rigor to our decision-making. It's going to be a challenge."

"Try to get some sleep, Hon."

"I won't be able to sleep. Got any other ideas?"

Epilogue

February 2008

Charlie was in a miserable mood. Truth be told, she'd been awful to be around for a couple of months and she knew it. One reason for her funk was seasonal affective disorder. She'd never been treated for the condition, but her mood always drooped when every single day was a cold, gray, dry-air assault to the soul, skin, and sinuses. That was a Detroit winter. However, the lion's share of Charlie's bitchiness could be attributed to losing Gil. He had moved to Washington, DC, with his wife in December. She missed him as a colleague and a friend.

In the past six weeks, Charlie and Don had interviewed a half-dozen people for the open partner position, but everyone fell short of filling Gil's shoes. For the second time Charlie asked Mandy to consider leaving the Grosse Pointe Park police to become a full-time private investigator. Mandy pointed out, again, the difficulties she thought they'd have navigating both a personal and professional life together. Charlie knew she was right.

"Are you sitting here in the dark for a reason?"

Judy didn't wait for Charlie's answer and flooded the conference room with light from overhead. She checked the coffee pot, decided it wasn't too strong, and poured a cup. "You want another?"

"Sure." Charlie rose to accept the coffee Judy poured, then enhanced it with two quick dollops of half-and-half. They stood for a moment enjoying the smooth jolt of caffeine.

"How do people live without coffee?" Charlie asked.

"Okay. Here's one I bet you don't know," Judy said.

"A Broadway song? About coffee? Oh boy!"

"Yep. It goes: *You're the cream in my coffee, dah-da-da-da-da-da.* I can't remember that part, but the rest is: *You will always be my necessity. I'd be lost without you.* It's a really old song."

Charlie laughed and returned to the table to sit. "How do you know this stuff?"

"My grandfather. I think he took me to every Broadway show from the time I was eight until I was fourteen."

"Amazing. What was the name of that show?"

"I don't remember. But at least I made you laugh. You've been a sourpuss for more than a month. It's getting old."

"I'm down because I miss Gil."

"Yeah. Me too. You haven't found anyone you like yet?"

"No. There were a couple of people who were okay, but Don didn't like them."

"What didn't he like?"

"They weren't tough enough."

Judy shook her head. "By the way, Don called. He's taking Rita to a doctor's appointment this morning. He'll be in this afternoon."

"Okay." Charlie could feel her dejection returning.

"What about somebody from Spectrum?" Judy asked. "Some of their guys seemed sharp. In fact, what about Cynthia? She'd be great."

Charlie sat upright. "Cynthia *would* be good, wouldn't she? She's organized, smart. She's not a lawyer but, remember, she really knew technology and seemed to work day and night. But I doubt she'd want to give up the auto show security duties. That's a really big job, and it pays a whole lot more than we can offer."

"It's worth a call, isn't it?"

"Do you still have her number, Judy? It's been two years since that investigation."

"I'm sure it's in the case file, but if I can't find it I know how to get it."

"Cynthia. That's a really great idea. I'd never have thought of that."

Judy pushed the manila folder she'd brought to the conference room toward Charlie.

"Inside are checks to be signed for our bills. Our new insurance policy is also in there. I've read it. Nothing's changed except, of course, the premium's gone up. Also, we got two more inquiries for domestic jobs. The phone slips are in there. I'll get you Cynthia's number."

"What's shaking, Mack?"

Don joined Charlie at the conference table and poked around in the always-present basket of cookies, crackers, candy and chips. He settled on a bag of M&M's.

"Everything okay with Rita's pregnancy?"

"Yeah. She's good. We had one of our regular appointments. Everything looks fine and we're still on track for a May delivery."

"Glad to hear it."

Charlie watched Don eat candy until he felt her eyes on him.

"What is it, Mack?"

"We need to talk."

"So, talk."

"I'm frustrated about not being able to find someone to replace Gil. It's been almost two months, and we need the help. I called Cynthia Fitzgerald today."

"From Cobo? She'd be a swell fit. Good thinking."

"It was Judy's idea."

"Okay. So, it was Judy's idea. What did Cynthia say?"

"She doesn't want the job."

"Well . . . too bad. It was a long shot. She makes more money than we could ever pay her, right?"

"Right." Charlie picked up her pencil to doodle on her legal pad. "Cynthia had another suggestion. A good one."

"Oh yeah?" Don was now working his way through a packet of cheese crackers.

"When Cynthia asked why I thought of her for the job, I told her because she was smart, organized, hard-working, good with technology, and nobody's fool."

"Right. She's all those things," Don said, plopping a cracker into his mouth.

"So is Judy."

Don choked so hard his face turned red. He stood, trying to dislodge the cracker from his throat. Charlie handed him a bottle of water. He took two big gulps.

"You can't be serious," Don bellowed.

Charlie closed the door of the conference room. "I *am* serious, Don. Will you hear me out?"

"There's nothing to hear. That's the worst idea you've ever come up with."

"I didn't come up with the idea. I told you, Cynthia suggested it."

"I don't give a damn whose suggestion it was. It's absurd. Judy cannot replace Gil. She doesn't have any of the skills to be an investigator." Don leaned back in his chair and folded his arms. "Bottom line. End of discussion."

Charlie began doodling. Don's default response to things he didn't want to hear was to hunker down in his opinion. If Gil were here, they'd come at Don from two angles. Usually, one of them would combine the right words or push the right button to get Don to reconsider his position. She knew she would need to keep him reeling with a combination of arguments and questions or, better yet, she could do her Post-it notes exercise.

Charlie stood and walked to the whiteboard. She erased the notes from yesterday's meeting and put a packet of green and red notes on the credenza. She tore off five green notes to jot down the facts, and lined them up from top to bottom on the left side of the board.

"What's that supposed to be?" Don grumbled.

"Here's what we know about Judy. Organized. Intuitive. Tech-savvy. Charismatic. Problem-solver."

Don shook his head. He wasn't playing along. Charlie wrote and posted two more green notes on the board.

"Innovative and trustworthy."

"What's she so innovative about? She labels and relabels those damned files every other day."

Don took another swig of water, and crossed his arms on the table. Charlie was making some headway. She peeled a red note from the packet, wrote a question on it, and leaned across the table to hand it to him. He sneered, shook his head, and finally reached for the note.

"Read it out loud," Charlie said.

"No," Don said, putting the note in the middle of the table.

"You don't have to read it aloud. You know it's true. It was Judy's ringtones idea that saved my life in the Birmingham case."

"It was just luck," Don countered.

"Oh yeah? Well what about this one?"

Charlie furiously jotted another question, then passed it to Don: "Wasn't it Judy who led us to the bombs in Cobo?"

Don dropped his eyes to the table. Charlie stood silently, letting him think. Finally, he looked up at Charlie. "Give me some of those notes."

Charlie shoved the green and red stickers his way and sat in the chair across from him. She watched him take her pencil and print first on the green pad, then write out a question on a red note. He slid them toward Charlie. The green note pointed out the fact that Judy wasn't an attorney. The red note asked: *What will Judy do when the shooting starts?*

"I've been thinking about whether or not we need another attorney. Only about 20% of our work requires a lawyer. If we have a client who really needs a lot of court procedural work, I'll do it or we can outsource it."

"What about this question?" Don snarled.

"It's true Judy is never going to pick up a gun. She doesn't even

200

like that part of our work, let alone is she trained for it. I concede your point. But how many times will we be in a firefight?"

"It's happened before," Don said. He didn't seem as angry.

"Judy can't be a replacement for Gil. But I don't know if anybody could. Maybe this is the time for us to rely on new skills, Don. Judy is really good on the phone. She could handle almost all of our background checks. We know her. She knows us. Nobody works harder."

"Have you already talked to her about it?"

"No. Of course not. I wouldn't do that before I conferred with you," Charlie said.

"Do you know if she would even want to be a partner? She'd have to put money into the business, just like we did."

"We can work something out. We should talk to her," Charlie said.

"Now?"

"Why put it off? Let's see what she says, and then we can all agree to sleep on it for a couple of days. What do you think?"

"I think you found a way to gang up on me. Even without Gil," Don said with a smirk.

Mandy got home from a night shift at eleven-thirty. She accepted the kiss and hugs from Charlie and Hamm, then went upstairs to lock her gun and take off her uniform. Fifteen minutes later she sank into the couch and stretched her legs across Charlie's lap.

"Hard evening?" Charlie asked, rubbing Mandy's knees.

"We raided a small-time drug operation. Mostly weed and pills, and we think some meth. It was a bunch of young guys. Maybe in their twenties. Bensen and I had to chase one of them a few blocks until the guy jumped over a fence and was attacked by a Doberman. It took the homeowner a bit of time to convince the dog to let go of the guy. We had to put the man in an ambulance. There was a bunch of back-and-forth with the homeowners, and then the paperwork back at the station. We had so much going on with the runner and the dog we missed all the action at the drug house." She wiggled her legs. "Oh, that feels wonderful," she said in response to the massage. "How were things at Mack Investigations today?"

"Don and I talked to Judy today about coming on as a partner."

"Judy." Mandy swung her legs to the floor. "Whose idea was that?"

"Cynthia Fitzgerald's."

"Wow. I'd never have thought of Judy. But it's a terrific idea, Charlie."

"I thought so too." Charlie laughed. "But it took some fast talking to get Don to even consider the idea."

"Oh, I bet," Mandy said. "Did you offer Cynthia the job?"

"Yes. She turned me down, but when I told her what qualities we were looking for, she reminded me that Judy had most of those skills."

"She's a keeper, all right. What did Judy say?"

"She was flabbergasted. It never even occurred to her to ask. She started crying."

"I'm sure that went over big with Don."

"I thought he was going to burst a vein. Anyway, I finally got both of them calmed down."

Mandy began laughing. Charlie joined in. Hamm, who was curled up and snoozing on the other end of the couch, opened his eyes and lifted an ear until the laughing subsided.

"One crying, and the other fuming. Your work is cut out for you," Mandy said. "So, Judy is Gil's replacement?"

"No. Like I told Don, we can't ever replace Gil. He had a unique combination of skills and qualities. You were the only one I thought could come close to filling his shoes with a minimum learning curve. But you turned me down."

"Twice." Mandy smiled.

"Yes, twice. Judy will bring a new set of skills. We'll have to make some adjustments at the office. We'll need a new office manager. Judy will be required to invest in the business, and she would work a trial period as a junior partner."

"That all sounds good."

Charlie's cell phone rang. Hamm lifted his head and both ears, and Mandy swung her legs to the floor.

"Is your phone upstairs?" Mandy asked.

"Yeah. It's charging. I wonder who could be calling this time of night?"

"Guess you better go find out," Mandy said, grabbing the tray with their empty tea mugs. "I'll lock up down here."

Charlie didn't recognize the number. *Telemarketers wouldn't call this late, would they?*

"Hello?"

"Hello. Is this Charlie?"

Charlie hesitated. Most people would answer this question straight out. She knew because it was a common technique when a private investigator was looking for someone.

"Who's calling?" Charlie asked with annoyance in her voice.

"Oh, I'm sorry. I know it's late. This is Pamela, uh, Pamela Rogers."

There was a pause on the phone.

"I'm sorry, I don't know . . ." Charlie began.

"Franklin's wife," the voice said.

Charlie had never met her ex-husband's new wife. Franklin had sent a pro forma wedding invitation to her mom, and had enclosed an extra invitation in the package for Charlie, but both Ernestine and Charlie had graciously RSVP'd their regrets.

Pamela Rogers *nee* Fairchild was a southeastern Michigan socialite with deep roots in the moneyed old families of the region. These were not old money familes, but nouveau riche from the Northeast who spread west to Michigan to keep an eye on their investments in the burgeoning auto manufacturing business. Not every one of these families had made money in cars, but they all managed to become wealthier when Detroit became America's Arsenal of Democracy during World War II.

"Charlie? Are you still there?" Rogers asked.

"Yes, I'm here. Just surprised to hear from you. We've never officially met."

"I know. I'm sorry."

"How is Franklin? Is anything wrong?" Charlie asked.

"Things are terribly wrong, Charlie. May I call you that? Everything is such a mess. I didn't know who else I could turn to."

"What's happened?" Charlie hoped her direct, forcefully asked question would calm the woman.

"Franklin's been charged with first-degree murder."

"What?"

"The police say he killed my brother last night. Charlie, I don't know where Franklin is. He hasn't called."

"Oh my God," Charlie said.

Mandy had come into the bedroom and now stood beside Charlie, touching her arm. "Is it your mom?" Mandy whispered with a worried face.

"No. Franklin is in trouble."

"Are you speaking to me?" Pamela said.

"No. I'm sorry. I was talking to my partner. What do you need me to do, Mrs., uh, Pamela? Did Franklin ask you to call me?"

"No. He'd be angry that I've called. But, my father said I needed some outside help. My father doesn't particularly care for Franklin, and he long ago gave up on my brother, but my mother is distraught. Daddy has to bring her back to Michigan next week to bury her son, and he wants to make sure the police aren't dragging their feet."

"Do you believe Franklin killed your brother?" Charlie continued her direct questions, and Mandy's grip on her arm tightened.

"No, I don't. He couldn't do such a thing."

"The police report is pretty clear, Mack," Don said. "They said your ex's gun was found on the floor, and there was some kind of a scuffle, and his fingerprints are all over the place."

204

"I don't care what the police say. Franklin doesn't have it in him to kill a man."

"Charlie, you said his current wife will pay us to investigate?" Judy asked.

"Yes. Pamela said, and I quote: 'We will pay you for your time, and pay you handsomely.'"

"Guess that means we have a case," Don said.

". . . and this will be Judy's first case as a private investigator, and junior partner."

"Heaven help us," Don said, ignoring the nasty glances the two women gave him.

Mack Investigations was back at full strength and on the job.

About the Author

A Detroit native, Cheryl A. Head now lives on Capitol Hill in Washington, DC. Her debut book *Long Way Home: A World War II Novel* was a 2015 Next Generation Indie Book Award finalist in the African American Literature and Historical Fiction categories. *Bury Me When I'm Dead* (Book One of the Charlie Mack Motown Mystery Series) was a 2017 Lambda Literary Award finalist, and included in the Detroit Public Library's African American Book list. In 2019, Head was inducted into the Saints & Sinners LGBT Literary Festival Hall of Fame. She also serves as the Director of Inclusion for the Golden Crown Literary Society.

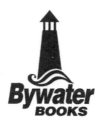

At Bywater Books we love good books about lesbians just like you do, and we're committed to bringing the best of contemporary lesbian writing to our avid readers. Our editorial team is dedicated to finding and developing outstanding writers who create books you won't want to put down.

We sponsor the Bywater Prize for Fiction to help with this quest. Each prizewinner receives $1,000 and publication of their novel. We have already discovered amazing writers like Jill Malone, Sally Bellerose, and Hilary Sloin through the Bywater Prize. Which exciting new writer will we find next?

For more information about Bywater Books and the annual Bywater Prize for Fiction, please visit our website.

www.bywaterbooks.com